CRITICAL ACCLAIM FOR THE TORN SKIRT

"A fast-paced and suspenseful narrative. . . . Fresh, with an original, idiosyncratic voice and keen observations of teenage angst. A powerful debut."

—Toronto Star

"Not since Sylvia Plath's *Bell Jar* has a young woman produced such a harrowing and literate first novel. Godfrey's Sara bristles with all the rebellion, apathy and self-destructiveness of a modern-day Esther Greenwood."

—Bruce LaBruce,
author of *The Reluctant Photographer*

"So evocative, so stunningly realized. . . . Compelling [and] authentic. . . . A daring debut."

—National Post

"A raw, intimate novel. . . . It feels as though a girl sitting next to you on the bus is showing you her diary. . . . *The Torn Skirt* exposes the fragile underbelly of adolescence."

—Quill & Quire

"Tremendously evocative. . . . [Godfrey] knows that everyday language is the secret of the great writer, and it grants her naked, Bellow-esque moments. . . . Godfrey's talent is established beyond doubt."

—Ottawa Citizen

"*The Torn Skirt* has enough drugs, parties, punks, and criminal behavior to convince most mothers that locking their little darling in the upstairs bedroom is the safest way to go. . . . A wild, edgy read."

—Times-Colonist

"Voice of the bad girls . . . [a] literary rebellion."

—Maclean's

Janet Johnson

About the Author

REBECCA GODFREY has written for *Detour*, *Index*, and other magazines. She holds an M.F.A. from Sarah Lawrence College, and lives in New York City. She is currently writing *Under the Bridge*, an account of a true high school murder case.

THE TORN SKIRT

Rebecca Godfrey

Perennial

An Imprint of HarperCollins*Publishers*

A previous edition of this book was originally published in Canada in 2001 by Harper-Collins Publishers.

First Perennial edition published 2002.

Designed by Too Kam

Library of Congress Cataloging-in-Publication Data
Godfrey, Rebecca.
     The torn skirt / Rebecca Godfrey.
          p.   cm.
     ISBN 0-06-009485-0
     1. Teenage girls—Fiction. 2. Victoria (B.C.)—Fiction. 3. Female friendship—Fiction. 4. Abandoned children—Fiction. 5. Parental deprivation—Fiction. I. Title.
PR9199.4.G63 T67 2002
813'.6—dc21   2002072579

02 03 04 05 06 ❖/RRD 10 9 8 7 6 5 4 3 2 1

THE TORN SKIRT

BLAME it on the Pleasure Family. Blame it on the Vietnam War. Blame it on a lot of things. But don't blame it on Justine. She was just a weak, scared girl; a lost, violent girl. A lot of things, she was. Was.

Or don't blame it on anything. Call it inevitable, call it the doomed fate of love. Call it karmic, fucked up, the dance of the wolves. Live it, love it, call it life. Call it Led Zeppelin. Yeah, yeah. Really, I don't really, really don't fucking care.

*　*　*

I was born with a fever, but it seemed to subside for sixteen years. High school, I was a good girl. I was pretty, I smiled, I fit in fine. And then as I turned sixteen and stopped smiling, the fever returned, though my skin stayed pale and sure, showing no sign of the heat inside me. 102 degrees, it returned for no reason. It returned around the time I met Justine, but blame it on her bad influence and you'd be all wrong.

I come out into the kitchen, have my little chat with the cop. Unsmiling, I get to him. I'm sure of it. All the teen girls on this hick island have flipped-back Farrah Fawcett hair, willing-to-please eyes shadowed in baby blue. Me, in my little shredded dress and desecrated eyes. I don't shock him, but I'm not what he hoped for. He writes something in his pad.

Teenage Girl. Angst-Ridden. Badly Dyed Hair.

The cop, thirty or so, with a mustache and the dullest eyes, doesn't ask about Justine. He asks what time I expect my mother back.

"Is that relevant to the case?"

"*Relevant?* That's a big word for a little girl."

Suddenly, I'm nauseous. I'm reeling. I'm realizing all the things I don't have words for. The world for him a pad of dates, names, serial numbers, license plates. He'd need a soundtrack for his report, a rush of images: her legs alone, her legs kicking backwards, the slit of her skirt ripping as she ran, her legs like wishbones.

Some more notes in his pad now; I imagine them.

Single-Parent Family. Headed by Father. That Crazy Diehard Hippie.

And get this: the cop is checking me out. I thought the sight of me might disgust him, but I should have known. Just because

I'm soft-skinned and sixteen, they get this sick, weak look.
Speed kicking in, not making me mellow, lazy, hazy, and high.
Making me violent and blue, restless and aware of all the things
I've got to do. All the things I've got to do.

"Touch my forehead," I tell him.

He does this, with little hesitation.

"You're hot."

"Yeah, I seem to be coming down with a bit of a fever."

"Maybe you should lie down and we can talk in your room."

"This whole thing has been very disturbing for me."

"I'm sure it has been," he says. "*Disturbing*, that's a good
word."

He stands up. Moves toward me.

"I have a fever," I tell him. "You'd better stay away."

I head for my bedroom, and hear him walking away past the
marijuana plants that line my father's shelves.

He's left my house and gone to jerk off, I bet. Jerk off in the
front seat of his cruiser. I'm in my bedroom and he's imagining
me here. A little girlyworld of Maybelline and heartthrobs
Scotch-taped above pink pillows. Really, it's a bare room of
white walls and Justine's books and skirts scattered all over the
floor.

I try to sleep, but sleep's not easy when you're on speed. I
guess the cop never left because now he's knocking on my
door. I ask him to leave; I tell him I'm too hot to talk. Fuck. He
says we must, but I won't. Just laughing at the thought of him
banging down the bedroom door of a teenage girl. He imagines
it pink and soft. He has no idea.

IN THE BUSHES WITH THE BURNOUT BOYS

I GUESS all this shit started when I was in the bush. I loved the bush. Behind our school, it was like some tangled, rising creature, hands reaching skyward; a thousand savage, skinny fingers. Evergreens and Scotch pines twisting with blackberry bushes and dead oaks. Mornings before school, I used to head into it with my stupid Swiss Army knife. Hack and chop a path leading into a clearing. And at lunch hour, I'd bring the burnout boys in.

I'm not making this up: the burnout boys all had one-syllable names: Bryce, Bruce, Dean, and Dale. They were only a bit wayward, but they thought they were real rebels. Bragging as they brought out their plastic baggies of mushrooms and weed.

May: the bush was rainsoaked; we were whacked around as we went in. I lifted branches back, holding them so the burnouts could enter. We sat on the ground, in a dry place, hidden from the concrete slab of our school. Here, the mountains faded from view. The blue sky went white.

It began to rain again, the pale, common May rain. I sat down on the dirt, lay back with my hair on a broad, mossy rock. The air smelled great at this moment—it smelled like rot and rain and Christmas.

Bryce drove his red pickup truck to the bush and opened the front door. Twelve o'clock: the Power Hour. Burnouts loved the Power Hour. Heaven. For them. They know every word. They sang along, pretending guitars were in their hands. They sang the Lemon Song to me.

Squeeze me baby so the juice runs down my leg.

My father used to say his generation fucked up in a lot of ways, but at least they invented rock and roll.

You can have it, I'd say. But the burnouts want it. They raised their fists in my clearing, sang the Lemon Song. They looked pretty hilarious.

What's so funny?

She's just high, Dean said, though they all knew I never smoked pot. I couldn't click with that giggly, slow, stupid state of being.

No, I said, I'm not high. I'm—

Laughing at you is what I was about to say.

Dean Black covered my knee with his hand. A light pat.

What's so funny, Ice Queen?

Everyone at school called me Ice Queen. There was always someone telling me to smile and not look so stuck-up.

I could feel moss catching in my hair. I wanted to go back to class with the dirt under my fingernails; rain streaking my mascara; a crown of twigs and moss. I hoped Dean Black would lift the steely brown brambles from my red hair.

Dean Black's the headcase; the heartthrob; the one I'm

supposed to love. He's got silky, shoulder-length hair, an Afro comb tucked in his Bootlegger jeans. He wants to be a rock and roll star, but he'll settle for planting trees. After he receives a diploma from Mount Doug—or Mount Drug, as it's known—he'll go up to Horsefly Lake. That's where the logging companies have cut down all the trees, thrown down napalm, burned and slashed the stumps. In the charred black ground, kids like Dean will plant sprigs. They'll earn ten cents a tree. He's seen me with my Swiss Army knife, hacking off branches. He thinks I should come with him. He smiles bratty when he talks about treeplanting; his grin's crooked and pure. He wants me to come and sleep in his tent, but I can't imagine him in a cremated forest. I can't even imagine him carless. I can only see him as he is. The guy who drives to the liquor store and walks in without fear. Bottle in hand, bounding back to the car, raising his arms and bellowing, *We are the champions.* He'd slide up the window, put his hands up my shirt, and swig Southern Comfort. His hands up my shirt, he'd sigh kindly. He really wasn't a bad guy. Especially when he was alone. I'd bring him down to Arbutus Cove. We'd lie in the crevice where the curve of rock was still damp from the tide. Grappling like we were in the black water, blind and floating, he'd get nervous. I didn't want him to move away from me and reach for his prized plastic bag. I'd tease him. Offer to take off my top if he threw his drugs in the water. A hard choice for a burnout. Don't make me do this, he'd say, and then he'd give in.

I thought I was on to something.

Lying in the crevice with him, I could forget about treeplanting and living on an island where the ocean surrounded me, always.

In the bushes, he's different. I can't tell him how much I hate the music on his radio, how familiar lazy days, loud guitars, and slow, stoned laughter are to me. I've known all this since I was a kid, but to him it was new and fresh, a real risk. His mother had sewn Led Zeppelin's logo on the back of his jacket, in gold thread. His father was the manager of Canadian Tire, which made Dean the wealthiest kid in our school. Except for Ivy Mercer, and no one talked to her. She had a haughty stare and hid out in the library. Maybe later I'd make another feeble attempt to befriend Ivy, but for now I was in the bushes with the burnouts.

And then Heather Hale walked by.

As always, she was in tight jeans and had perfectly curled hair. Blond wings framed her face; she had a ski-jump nose and a slight limp. Heather Hole, they called her. I liked her, but she never seemed to have much to say to me. She walked by the bush, avoiding the clearing. I could see her, heading for the subdivision cul-de-sac.

Heather walked like an old man, as though she was slowly going blind, unsure of her step.

Dean whistled, put his hand on my knee in that shut-up kind of way.

Hey hose, he said.

Hey garden hose, Bruce said.

Dale made a motion near his crotch, as if he was whipping a snake around.

Heather kept walking, but I saw her wilt. Wilt and crumple. God, get her some oxygen, I almost said. She was a tough stoner girl. She had a leather purse full of silver-foiled balls of hash and stolen Maybelline. Once, she'd changed her tampon in front of me while sipping her father's gin. But now I knew she was soft. She should have known better. She had this soft, hurt look as she limped by.

What's the garden hose? I asked. Heather had gone into her

car, but I couldn't see her face. Her windshield was covered with rain.

They answered me, probably only because a question from me caught them off guard.

So, lucky me, sitting in the enchanted forest, missing math class. Getting to hear all the details of how they'd spent Friday night putting a garden hose up Heather. After they'd gone there. Dean, Dale, Bryce, Bruce. One by one. Then they washed her out, washed her clean. *She was really clean, man, she was so wet.* And she loved it, they said, she loved the way we cleaned her.

Dean broke a branch with his hands as Bryce spoke. Bryce spoke, I wouldn't say proudly. He spoke of the garden hose incident like it was a distant fun break, a video game. I kept looking at Dean, and I really didn't know what to do because I didn't know if this was normal, if burnout idiots did that shit all the time because they read in *Hammer of the Gods* that Robert Plant did the same thing to a groupie. I got up. I didn't feel the fever, but I felt a warmth, like a thousand fists slamming up against taut skin. A hidden current you find, but what good is it? What do you do with it? I had no idea.

So that was the end of my little love affair with Dean Black. I went back inside the school and spent the rest of math class in a toilet stall, staring at my veins and reading the bad poetry on the wall. *If you love something, set it free. If it comes back, it was always yours.* Someone had scrawled over the last words, so it now read, *If you love something, set it free. If it comes back, SHOOT IT.*

Heather Hale came into the girls' room. I recognized her white pumps; she always wore them with white ankle socks. Through the gap under the door of the stall, I watched her hands franti-

cally rubbing dirt off her white pumps. I could hear water running, and her voice saying ShitShitShit as she went down once
more with the paper towel, scrubbing her muddy heels. I
thought if I went out, she might cry, and I would have to comfort her. Not having a mother around, you're frightened when
you have to hug and console and do all those motherly things. I
didn't want to have to comfort her.

But she wasn't crying. She was staring in the mirror, putting
on lip gloss.

I'm so sorry about that, I said.

She looked startled. She backed away from me. She fumbled
with something in her purse.

Sorry about what? she said. Her voice was soft, breathless.

That garden hose thing.

She kept looking in the mirror. She covered her freckles with
foundation.

It was just sex, she said. They wanted to do it so I let them.
She shrugged her shoulders.

I didn't smile, though she smiled at me. She shrugged her
shoulders again. Erase this, she seemed to be saying, erase,
erase, erase. I thought, Fine, disappear before my eyes.

*   *   *

Did I handle that right? I really didn't know what to do. When I
got home from school, I went straight for the wild garden
behind our house and looked for Seamus, but he wasn't around.
There was a large apple tree at the back of our garden, and he'd
put my rusted tricycle up in the boughs as some kind of monu-
ment to my former days as a toddler adventuress.

I wished Everly was around. I hadn't thought about her for a
long time, really. Hey, Mom, should a girl care if a guy sticks a

garden hose up her and laughs about it the next day? I doubted she'd know. Maybe she got into that kind of thing too. After all, she'd left me and Seamus for the leader of the Pleasure Family.

When he walked in that night, I stayed in my bedroom, looking at some pictures of models I had torn from magazines. Some glossy good girls. I could hear him, busy, in the kitchen. He might be rolling a joint, sealing the edges of white paper with the roselike tip of his tongue.

You OK, honey? he yelled to me. Got to give him credit. He never told me to smile; he never came into my room.

I went out and sat silent at the kitchen table. He looked like a little bald Buddha in blue overalls. Rhubarb was boiling over, staining the white stovetop I'd just scrubbed. He started talking about the Trees. I didn't really listen. I'd heard this speech before. The Trees of Eden. The Trees of Paradise. Soon as it was summer he would go up to Tofino. He said, in the forests, he'd build a house with his own hands. He thought I should come with him and learn the crucial skills of carpentry. I couldn't tell him I had no interest in carpentry.

I would never tell him that.

He was all I had, and he'd done so much for me. He had a good heart. Who could fault him? I guess we were close, but not close enough for me to say, What do you do when you go to a school where girls get a garden hose stuck up in them and smile like they need no comfort?

Seamus and I ate rhubarb soup in front of the TV. Our TV. We had this neighbor who was always giving us stuff. Toasters and hair dryers, a TRS-80, and now the TV. I guess he thought we should get into the electronic age.

Ronald Reagan was on TV smiling in a cowboy hat. He looked like one happy cowboy.

I'll get you, Seamus was saying. He went over to the screen.
I'll get you, he said, and he tapped the screen.

Dad.

He was pretty high. I don't think he noticed.

Ronald Reagan kept on smiling.

*   *   *

That garden hose thing was really getting to me. I don't know
why. I didn't want to go back to school. What I wanted to do
was walk around where there was no one my age. No burnouts,
no preppies, no jocks, no bops, no nature kids, none of those
stupid divisions. It was funny because then I thought of the
fever. Though I hadn't had a high temperature since I was a kid,
I could almost remember the way my body burned.

I thought maybe I should get a health note and just stay away
from school for a few days till I felt calmer and could smile
again. Maybe I'd even start smoking pot, mellow out and relax.
Some stoner boys and me would suck on a fat joint. We'd suck
the smoke till it was deep in our throats, and then we'd laugh
and laugh. The stoner boys would turn to me and I'd be stoned
out of my head. They'd say, Sara, you're so sweet. You used to
be the Ice Queen, but now you're so sweet and kind.

I could never fake a fever, though. I have one of those faces.
Call it innocent, though it's obviously not. One of those faces.
You know. The kind that never lets you lie.

Seamus turned off the TV and embraced some package. It was
wrapped in brown paper, and my father's name was surrounded by hand-drawn hearts. You'd think it was from some
teenage girl with a shameless crush. But it was from Sylvia, his
girlfriend. When she was in our house, she wafted around all

pepperminty. She made me earrings. Crystal triangles, she said, carried love from the sun. I couldn't stand her.

Got your knife? Seamus asked me. He was struggling with Sylvia's knots of twine.

He had his own knife. Still, he liked to use mine.

He had some kind of sentimental deal with my knife. It was a gift for my birthday when I turned fourteen. He thought I loved it, and maybe I did—then. I'd been elated by the sight of the Eaton's box. Finally, I thought, he's giving me something from a store. He's giving me a girl's prize: Barbie, a jewelery box with a ballerina, some china heart on a silver chain. A gift that wouldn't smell of dirt or his hardworking hands. Maybe I loved the knife; at least it was brand new and it shone.

I couldn't feel the cold clasp of my knife. I told him I didn't have it.

He looked really worried. You need that knife, he said. It'll come in handy.

Yeah, I'll get it tomorrow, I said. I knew it was in the clearing with the burnouts and I wasn't gonna go back there ever again.

Good, he said, and he tousled my hair. He went down to the basement to get his own.

I put my hand up my shirt, just to make sure. Though I was pretty sure. I'd kept the knife in my bra since I'd had a bra. I could feel the white cloth and my skin and my breast and nothing else. So fuck the knife.

It was funny to keep something so close to you and then you have no need for it after all.

It would stay undiscovered and useless in my clearing, lying in the dank dirt with trodden twigs and spit-soaked roaches. It would rust unnoticed as the clearing grew over and the entrance was barred by branches because who would cut it if I didn't.

Fuck It Up

MING'S is a small Chinatown grocery store with a diner in the corner. I sat near a long, black electric sign. The sign constantly flashed the winning lotto numbers in a digital blur. Though the sky was still dull with fat clouds, the view from the window of Ming's was red. Red, the dragons licking at a turquoise sun on a fading old building across the street, their red tongues turning to red flames. Red of neon letters flashing Kwon Tung, red of the garbage cans, and even the telephone booth a red temple. Red like some slutty nail polish gracing the fingers of a girl whose hands make you think of blood and stop signs.

I was just basically hanging out, hiding out at Ming's. If I had some friends, maybe I would have celebrated my big brave act. Skipping school. But I'd lost my friends, and I couldn't really convince myself that I was brave. I'd handled the garden hose incident with such little finesse. So I was just hiding out at the corner counter, me and two out-of-work logger guys. You can always tell a logger. They smoke Export A's and wear woolen jackets in the spring. These loggers beside me at Ming's were out of work and complaining about it. They were talking about driving to Cowichan to clearcut; they were trying to remember the name of Dennis's wife. Dennis's wife knew the foreman, but what the fuck was her name. They were burly guys, and sitting next to them I felt sort of safe and silly at the same time. There were no tourists at Ming's, no teenage kids. I could hide there forever. This town's small enough so you always see someone you recognize. But not at Ming's. The loggers beside me began to talk about dog food.

I thought I should start thinking about how I should get it together. Get it together soon. Maybe move to New York, become a model, begin an exciting life. It seemed ridiculous, but girls in magazines were always doing it. And I'd even had this one guy saunter over to me like I'd handed him an invitation. So sure of himself, he came right up to me. He looked like an idiot lech but he said he was a scout. How old are you? Is that the real color of your hair? Has anyone told you you could be a model? I wanted to tell him to fuck off, but he probably thought he was being polite. I still had his slimy card around somewhere; I thought maybe I should give him a call.

I took out my notebook, telling myself to make a list of all the things I wanted to accomplish before I turned seventeen. But the problem with me was that as soon as I started thinking about getting it together, I got this mad craving desire to fuck it up.

No one served me at Ming's. I didn't know what was going on. In the kitchen, a small man's head was swaddled in steam. Our eyes met, he nodded, but he stayed in the steam. The loggers were helping themselves to coffee, just grabbing the pot right off the counter. I wanted a root beer. My throat was dry and I had a bad sugar urge. Lately, it seemed either I got a lot of attention or I was completely ignored. One or the other, but nothing in between. I wondered if the loggers knew who my father was. I was afraid they'd start joking about him. That goddamn crazy hippie called me a murderer just 'cause I chainsaw trees. I hated hearing people laugh about my father. But I didn't really care.

The empty pages of my notebook glared at me like I was some kind of traitor. *What are you gonna do? Come on. Let's see some motivation, some ambition, some brilliant plan.*

I sat there, staring at the street. Pretending I was real exotic. To do this, I had to deny a few facts.

Our Chinatown was only one street. And maybe the street was great, with sleazy show-off neon and murder red everywhere, but I'd seen fashion spreads in magazines. New York or Toronto: their Chinatowns veered and swerved, mobbed with people rushing around their thrilling lives, rushing and pushing their way through a tangled maze of maybe two hundred streets.

Some guys in the back of Ming's were looking at skin mags. That was how I first heard about Ming's. These fat guys on the bus were talking about how they'd go to Ming's to look at the skin mags because there was no chance of anyone like the little lady or the baby-sitter walking in on them. This one guy was saying once he'd been at Book World looking at Hustler, and his daughter came in to buy Bop. You should go to Ming's, the other guy said. You know, the chink store. It's always empty; they've got a lot of skin mags. No one comes in but a greasy chink now and then.

Once, when I was fifteen, I wandered back there. I saw some comic books, and a few ancient issues of Chatelaine, and rows and rows of skin mags. I took a little look; I just sort of glanced around, and then I bought some firecrackers for my former boyfriend Dean Black. Now I just turned my head and glanced back there. I could see three men, trying not to touch each other, as they leaned forward, reaching and opening and gazing.

I wondered what they thought of me, a tall girl with messy hair and a notebook blank of goals. You should have seen the way I dressed then. It was pretty unsexy. I was wearing long johns and my father's flannel shirts, one wrapped around my waist to hide the baggy crotch on my white thermal underwear. I looked overbundled. Wearing my father's shirts meant I didn't get hassled by the hallway critics at school—those thicknecked football fucks who sat in the foyer rating girls as they went by. When I had some money and got out of Victoria, I thought I'd start dressing like the models in magazines. Magazines were always going on and on about Your True Style, and I thought I probably had some true style, but it would have to wait till I was There. You know what I was thinking when I caught sight of those men in the corner looking at skin mags? I had this sudden, horrifying idea that Everly, my mother, was in those magazines. It was a possibility, but not one I wanted to consider, so I turned back to my smirking notebook. The Pacific Ocean surrounds my island, and it's something I'd never crossed, something cold and endless which kept me away from the rest of the world. It was like a chaperone; a constant presence reminding me that I couldn't wander away. My blank pages gave me the same feeling as the ocean. *Sara, you're not going anywhere.*

My presence at the corner counter didn't stop the men from looking at skin mags; I don't think they even knew I was there.

A skinny girl came in. She slammed open the door, and a cluster of silver bells smashed against glass. She was frail and looked a bit unhealthy, but she seemed unaware of this. She walked like she was a star in certain select circles, so it didn't matter what anyone outside of those circles thought of her. She walked fast and straight.

The loggers sneered. *What the hell's that?*

I guess it's Halloween early, eh?

Ha, if I was her father, she'd be over my knee.

As she walked back to the men staring at skin mags, I could see the slit in her tight skirt was torn. She stood beside the men. I hadn't seen her face; I had no idea how old she was. She could have been twelve. She grabbed a fat little comic book. I thought standing back there was a pretty stupid thing to do. They might think you were like those girls they were gazing at; the one with her legs spread and the stupid caption: *Julie loves chasing butterflies.* They might touch you.

Her voice was rough and sweet. She nudged him with her elbow, the guy beside her. She showed him her comic book. *What do you think of Betty?* she asked.

He ignored her; she stood beside him, a little too close. After a few seconds, he was up at the counter, clutching a *Chatelaine*. No one at the cash register, so he threw some bills on the counter.

I couldn't take my eyes off her. Slim-hipped, roving, she came up to where I was.

She came up to the counter and pocketed the money the man had left for a magazine.

Ming!

The small man came out of his kitchen. His face was damp and old, but he smiled when he saw her.

I put away my notebook.

You stay down here, he said, you stay off Yates Street. Your probation lady told me. The Red Zone stops here.

The Red Zone, she said, yeah, yeah.

Everyone in this town hates you, he said. I heard.

Thanks a lot, she said. She had a toothbrush around her neck; it was hanging from a small pink chain. She stuck it in between her lips like the dirty bristles were some kind of candy.

Look at your skirt, he said. You can't sew.

Who cares, she said.

You want some food? he asked kindly. Stay here. Stay in Ming's.

He gave her an egg cream. She left the straw wrapped and sucked on the creamy froth. She crossed her legs and glanced at me. I could see how hacked her hair was, badly dyed from blond to black. She pushed the ragged strands from her face, as if she wanted to show off her full lips and clear blue eyes.

She smiled at me and I turned away, as though I'd been found out.

Another man from the magazine stand came up to the counter. He threw down some magazine called Jailbait. My mother could be in Jailbait. She'd been arrested once. She had a police record. She didn't do anything really cool to earn it. She didn't rob a bank or anything. She just sat in some field and refused to move.

The skinny girl put her hand on the man's money. Ming must have been blind; he looked at her lovingly and grinned.

She began singing his name: Ming, Ming, oh Ming. You going to come see me when I have a band, Ming? I'll sing your song. Ming, Ming, oh Ming.

No, no, he said. No song for Ming.

Oh come on, she said, everyone wants a song.

Not Ming, he said. Ming wants no song.

She looked bored. She paid for some cigarettes with the money she'd stolen.

She walked out, singing, Ming, Ming, Ming.

No song, he said.

What was her name? I asked him.

He hesitated, sizing me up. Justine, he said quickly. And then he walked back into his kitchen.

The dirty steam rose like fog lifting.

I followed her out. I don't know why. What else was there to do? The fog turned to rain, and in the rain her torn skirt became transparent. I could see the line of her legs and the bones in her back. We left the red street and walked by drab gray two-story buildings with flat roofs. In the distance, I could make out the harbor, dwarfed by mountains and the masts of sails. The buildings beside me seemed pathetic by comparison, shoddy and doomed. A sign in the window of a furniture store said, CONGRATULATIONS! WE'RE GOING OUT OF BUSINESS! THANKS FOR YOUR SUPPORT!

Yates Street was a street where people congregated; it was where all the buses picked up and dropped off. She turned onto Yates Street and slowed down near the welt in the street where a store must have burned down. There was this big crater in the concrete; it looked horrific.

I really had nothing to do on Yates Street. I couldn't catch a bus home. I didn't live in Oak Bay or Royal Oak or Cadboro Bay or Cordova Bay, those quiet, gardeny places. Still, I sat down on a bench, as though waiting for a bus.

I watched her enter a dark, narrow alley. I didn't know about the Red Zone yet. I just thought it was an alley, and she ran into it. It was funny to see someone run on a street downtown. I could see the tear in her skirt widen, and her heels kick off the ground, and she was gone. Then the alley was empty, and I could see the rain and the space like a hole.

Wherever she was running, I knew it wasn't to a collapsing home with a pothead father or into the bushes with the burnout boys. Watching her run, I thought, Down is somewhere. You didn't have to ascend off the island like some magazine model; you didn't have to push yourself through veering, crowded, exotic streets. You could just slash through a shortcut, heading down, and the sky would stay like a hole.

Heat kicked through me then, a burning, dizzy sift of heat. No one around me would have noticed. No one would have known my freakish malady had returned, the fluke of my faulty body. My skin stayed pale; I didn't faint. All this time, I'd been worried about my father being killed by a drunk logger, and suddenly I was the one who might die. Die on Yates Street surrounded by old ladies. Dear, they'd say, sweetie, what is wrong with you? They'd call the doctor; haul me off. Seamus would come in screaming about how he didn't want me to be cared for by chemists with their man-made medicines.

So I willed my fever away. Swooning with stupid heat, I thought of Alaska; the shade of towering trees.

And walking home, I hoped the warmth was really regret. My fear; my cowardice. The moment at Ming's, the moment on the street, any moment when I could have spoken to the skinny girl. But instead, I'd kept a distance and watched, no better than a lech looking for fresh prey. Only it wasn't fear as much as certainty. I was certain I knew what she'd think of me. She'd hate me for being pretty and overbundled, poor, friendless, more or less a mute, a mute with no plans. She'd hate me for being known around high school as an Ice Queen, a girl who couldn't help Heather after she'd had a garden hose stuck up her by Dean Black and his burnout brigade. Walking by some sweet old ladies, heading for the blue bridge that would bring me home, I knew. How she'd hate me. Just hate me.

THE GET LAID

THE last block of Yates Street looks like it could be in a Western. There's old brick buildings left over from when Victoria was a gold rush town. They have high false fronts and entrances with heavy stone archways. The King's Hotel is an old gunslinger saloon where all the loggers go to get trashed.

I should have walked, even run, by the derelict old hotel. Should have raced right by the skanky diner, a twenty-four-hour dive called the Day and Night.

But I swear, when I swerved into the diner, all I wanted was to splash some cold water on my face.

Lurid lights washed over me. God, please don't let me faint, I thought. I wasn't seeing things straight and clear; I'd glance before I'd veer. I saw the inside of the diner as if I was down on my back and a strobe light was flashing everything into slivers above me. Flash of a painted cowboy. Flash of a sign: Introducing our FAMOUS Texas Steak Delight. Flash of a waitress wearing white orthopedic shoes.

I smelled rancid grease, meat, and Mr. Clean.

Later, I found out the diner had a bad rep as a teenage hooker hangout. That's why no one called it the Day and Night. Later, I found out that they called it the Get Laid and Fight.

In a burgundy booth there were two men sitting together. One of them was Braun Stewart. He was the modeling man, and under the harsh lights, he looked creepier than when I first saw him in sunlight. His skin was pockmarked; it looked sore and pierced. He was wearing a three-piece white suit, but even a blazer and vest couldn't make that guy classy.

His friend, Stanley, was short and pudgy with these strange, flabby lips. I know that sounds rude, but really, his lips looked like they could get up and waddle around all on their own. He was wearing a baseball cap that said Truckers Do It on the Road.

They were quite the pair, those two. Sitting together, snickering as they turned the pages of a magazine. When I walked by them, Braun called out to me.

Red, he yelled. Hey, Red. Red, red, red.

Fluorescent lights were scalding my face and the walls shuddered and I thought at any moment I was likely to puke.

I slouched over to their booth because I didn't really know what else to do. I kept my distance, though; I didn't want to get too close. Older men make me nervous. They always act like they've got something on you. Especially those two.

This is Stanley, Braun said, pointing at the shrively twerp. He's just leaving. Stanley, this is Sara. She's quite something, eh? I tried scouting her the other day.

I was surprised that the modeling guy remembered my name.

Sorry, I said, I'm not feeling well. I just want some water.

You look fine.

Well, I'm not fine. I'm—

Dying, I was about to say.

But instead, I just stood there, hovering at the edge of their table. Like a pair of flesh inspectors, they stared up at me. Sweat, I could feel sweat trickling down my back. The floor was covered with footprints, a pattern of black smears that reminded me of cavemen drawings. I looked down at the dirty pattern for a few minutes, and then I looked at the wallpaper, which was all cracked, and then I looked at a leak in the ceiling letting in a line of rain.

The two men kept staring at me, even though I'd never felt so ugly.

A country song was playing on the radio. I didn't know who was singing. John Wayne or one of those corny '50s guys.

From behind the curtain of hair covering my eyes, I mumbled, I was just thinking about you.

I don't know why I said that.

What were you thinking? Braun asked.

I'm trying to get off this island, and I thought maybe you'd have some advice.

Smart girl, he said.

Very smart, Stanley repeated. Then they both smiled their slithery smiles, and I saw Stanley's pink tongue. Lizardlike, he licked his bottom lip.

Sara, sit down, have a coffee.

They didn't ask me why I wasn't in school.

You wanna get your life together, then this here's your man. He's a very important man. Braun finds girls, Stanley said.

Where? I said, in a voice stupid and curious and shy.

Well, I find them in shopping malls and soccer fields, Braun said. He winked at Stanley. It's a tough job.

I thought it sounded like a weird job. Driving around, finding underage girls. It sounded like it should be illegal.

Anyway, I didn't care about modeling. Just because I was young and dull, they thought I had what it took to be a glossy good girl in magazines. Maybe I hoped so yesterday—but yesterday was a year ago. Now I just wanted to fuck things up. That was all I wanted, really.

She's a snob, Braun said. That's why she won't sit down.

A beautiful snob, Stanley said, but a snob nonetheless.

They both snorted, and Braun threw me this glance that meant *We're on to you.*

I'm not a snob.

You're just creeps, that's what I wanted to say.

Oh, you're not a snob, eh? Then why don't you sit down? For two seconds. Come on.

Come on, Stanley said. We're not going to bite.

If I didn't move soon, I would die. The heat in my body was waning, but I still felt dizzy and clammy, the way you feel waking up with a hangover or after falling asleep in the sun. How could they not tell? Fever's invisible. Too bad I wasn't born with leprosy.

Persuasion is a strange thing. Coercing, convincing, call it what you want. They say you should, really should, come across the street to a calm, classy, well-lit white studio. It's there that Stanley, professional photographer extraordinaire, will take a few Test Shots. That's all. And here's how they try to convince you.

They make you think that if you don't go, you're to blame for being a snob. You think you're too good for us? Come on! Why wouldn't you want to be photographed by Stanley here? His work's appeared in *Chatelaine* and *Flare*. He's top-notch. Come on! Bring your mother if you want. We'll send your photos to Elite. You could be in New York next week.

What do I have to do?

Smile. All you have to do is smile.

It sounds so simple. To them.

But I can't smile. Ask me why and I'll tell you. A girl I know just got a garden hose stuck up her, and the boys who did it were my friends, my only friends.

Just smile, Braun said.

Smile, Stanley said. Show us what you've got.

I tried to smile, but my lips refused. They faltered, falling, close to a frown.

I knew they were both likely to start laughing at me, so that's why I raised my chin and looked toward the back of the restaurant. Sunlight slanted through slats of the venetian blinds—the girl I saw seemed to be surrounded by a warm shadow. Her blond hair was feathered and she had a ski-jump nose.

It was Heather! If those two hadn't been staring so hard at me, I swear I would have screamed.

LOVE'S BABY SOFT

HEATHER was French-kissing an American sailor. Soon as she stopped, I realized she wasn't Heather after all, and I had a sudden urge to cry. Don't ask me why. Heather wore a lot of makeup, but this girl was even more heavy with the Maybelline. With her blue eye shadow and pink cheeks, she still managed to look wild and rowdy and a little wasted.

Give me a hamburger! she screamed raspily. Then she crashed into the sailor's arms. She punched his shoulder, and he lit her cigarette.

Hey, I said to Braun, that's a friend of mine over there. I've got to go say hello.

That is not a friend of yours, Stanley said.

She is. She goes to my high school. You guys should go scout her.

Scout her? Braun said. You have got to be kidding.

But I wasn't kidding. If I saw a fierce, fighting girl like her in a magazine, I'd never want to turn the page. Do your goddamn job, I thought. Get her into the pages of every fashion magazine.

Braun looked really offended. That was another reason I didn't talk much. I was always offending people.

He sighed. I drank his water since he hadn't touched a drop. Then, as if I'd been in a desert for years, I reached down and grabbed Stanley's glass and drank all of his water as well. The stolen ice cube felt so good, better than candy. I wished I could order one hundred ice cubes and keep them pressed against my parched tongue.

Why in God's name would I scout her? Braun said.

She's prettier than me.

That may be so, but unlike you, she's lost the necessary innocence.

Unlike you, she's lost the necessary innocence.

Occupational hazard, Stanley said, and he snickered as if he'd just told a dirty joke.

What does that mean? I said.

It means, Braun said, leaning closer as if he wanted to slap me with his nose, it means that she's a hooker.

When he said that, I got this sudden urge to poke him with my corkscrew. Only I didn't have my Swiss Army knife anymore. If I had, I swear I would have corkscrewed the guy. That was a really mean thing to say.

She is not, I said.

Look at her coat, Stanley said. For Christ's sake.

What was wrong with her coat? It was a white fur coat and I thought it was sophisticated.

Once I saw a movie with a hooker. She was rough-skinned and thirty, always entertaining limousine men in her lacy negligee.

She's my age, I said loudly.

Calm down, they both said at once. Calm down, calm down, calm down.

But why should I?

Just because a girl skipped school and dressed with style, they thought she was a hooker and tried to stop me from befriending her.

I bet she knew Justine. They probably ran down alleys together, having more fun in five seconds than these two had had in their entire lives. I felt sorry for them. Really, I did.

Sara's so naive, Braun said.

So naive, Stanley said. It's cute.

I started to walk away, holding the glass in my hand like a roll of stolen money.

Oh, come on, Braun said, and he grabbed my empty hand, tried to pull me back by his side. But I wrestled out of his grasp and turned without saying good-bye. Fuck them. I hated their guts.

Now I walked straight toward her, doing my best to look unafraid. I was gonna sit down and befriend her. I wasn't going to fuck up this chance, this time. But by the time I'd reached her, the sailor was caressing her face.

I heard him.

Don't break, China, he said. Don't break.

So then I just headed for the bathroom, thinking, I was sixteen and no man had ever touched me that lovingly.

In the bathroom, I splashed cold water on my face. My face was still a lie. Naive, those fools said, though I'm obviously not.

I had just sat down on the tile when suddenly China came bursting in like a bull out of a cage.

Hey, man, she said, like she'd known me all my life. Nice long johns!

She pulled a bottle of Love's Baby Soft out of her tan leather purse.

You should have seen the way she cradled the bottle. As though it wasn't some girly pink perfume, but a soft and tender grenade.

Hey, man, she said again, and she wiped her nose. My friend thinks you're cute.

The sailor?

Yeah, the fucking pongo.

That was what we called the American sailors who parked their boats in our harbor and strutted around our streets as if we asked for their protection.

What's his name?

His name? I don't know, man. Joe Blow, John Doe. I don't know his fucking name.

He seems like a nice guy, I said. Really, he didn't seem that nice. But I just wanted to keep talking to her. She was like the rising rowdy moment of a party just before the cops arrive and send everyone home. I always liked girls who looked like they could lose control. Around them, I felt, at last, that there was something in the world I wanted to learn.

He thinks you look like Anne of Green Gables. The freckles, the red hair. Men love that shit.

I lay down and pressed my cheek into the cold floor. There was mold in the cracks, green like silt at the bottom of the sea.

She sat down beside me, the pink bottle pressed between her thighs. I wanted to touch her fur because it looked so soft and comfortable, and everything else in the diner, the tiles, the mirror, the stolen glass, all seemed so hard and cold.

She poured some Love's Baby Soft into her hands and then

dabbed the pink water between her breasts. Under the fur coat, she wore nothing, not even a bra.

Man, men love this shit, she said.

I wished she'd stop saying *man*.

You should come party with me and John. We're gonna go party at the fucking King's Hotel.

I felt warm; it wasn't the fever, though.

Come on, man, she begged, but not the way Stanley and Braun had begged, as if they expected something I could never give. Her pleading was really a promise. *I promise you'll have fun.*

What else are you gonna do? she asked me. Hang out with Braun? She spat on the tile.

You know Braun?

Sure, I know Braun. Personally, I think the guy's running a one-man jerk-off operation. But who asked me, right? He gets all the wannabe high school chicks going up to his "studio." Maybe they end up in *Seventeen*, like he says. I couldn't tell ya, man, 'cause I do not give a flying fuck about little girls and their cutesy magazines.

Do you know Justine? I asked nonchalantly, pretending I really didn't care one way or another. But my heartbeat was like a punch under my breast when I said her name.

Sure. Who doesn't know Justine? The girl is fucking insane, man. Did you hear about how she—oh fuck, I'm so thirsty.

She raised the bottle of Love's Baby Soft to her lips.

Do you dare me to drink this? Come on, dare me, man.

Isn't it poisonous?

It's perfume! Hey, if I drink this entire bottle, will you come and hang out with me at the King's?

She didn't wait for my answer; she raised the bottle of sweet perfume to her lips. She swallowed, and then she drank some more.

The sailor knocked on the door. China! he yelled.

China! She imitated him, her voice bratty and whiny. I thought again of how he had touched her face.

Is China your real name?

Yeah, right! Sometimes I say Bali or Tahiti. Men love that shit. China usually goes over good. I like it. It's exotic.

I wished I could keep her in the bathroom with me, discover what it was that Justine had done. But the sailor knocked again. Not really a knock. He slammed his fist against our door.

Come on, she said. She stood above me now, and her fingers dangled down like a rope. I let her lift me, lift me from the floor.

My father would be home soon, puttering around the kitchen in his overalls. I had no curfew, but still I always came home after school. I'd make sure he had deposited the day's earnings. I'd go over the bank balances and bills, because lately he was forgetting all kinds of things. Then he'd scream at the news while I did my homework on my bed because I could think better lying down, with the warm breeze drifting through the window, smelling like lilacs and willow trees.

I always used to go home right after school. Because I never would want my father to worry about me.

Maybe I'll meet you later, I said.

She spat on the mirror, and the spit fell down so her reflection was like a painting of a girl with a tear.

I'm feeling a little feverish, I said. Where will you be later? I'll find you. I promise.

I don't know where the fuck I'll be. I'll be at work, man.

Where do you work?

She sighed. She seemed to lose interest in me. She gave me The Look. The look meant: Go Back to High School. You're Not Tough Enough for Me.

I'll be at the King's, she said. Room fucking two thousand. Room goddamn eight million and seventy-three!

And then she was outside. I could hear the sailor saying, Good girl, and I could hear her giggling—a softer, desperate laugh so completely unlike the way she had laughed when she was with me.

My Lover, The Dirt

I ROLLED over onto my stomach and moved my hand under my shirt to see if my skin was still warm. My father's garden was a mess. There was no lawn, just patches of herbs and weeds underneath the wild flowering trees. Still, when I came home from the Day and Night, I went into the garden and thought there was nowhere I would rather be.

My body was warmer than it had ever been before.

I moved my hand down between my legs, wanting to push the feeling further, push it all the way inside, push it further and faster, faster and further, until I was there. The ground under me was rough, harder than any boy. My hips rocked up; I heard the long sound of my soft sigh.

Then someone was in the garden; I could hear footsteps behind the rosebush.

My face was still pressed against the dirt when I saw him.

My father. He stood a few feet away from me, a pair of silver scissors in his hands. He didn't finish his cutting; he just turned and headed down the dirt path leading to our house. I knew he'd seen me because I saw his eyes and they were guilty and terrified.

Brushing the dirt off my face, I rolled onto my back. I watched as the sky turned from gray to black, and the first few stars appeared. A breeze lifted through my hair, rustled through the trees.

I wanted to go to my bedroom, but I couldn't go into our home. How could I look at him? My poor father; he was probably only cutting flowers. Because he used to do that for me. When I came home from school, a vase of flowers would always be waiting on the worn-out white desk in my bedroom.

That night, there were no roses in my room. I threw my notebook on the floor and the pages fluttered open. The words I'd written in Ming's were even more mocking after my disastrous little chat with Braun. *Become a model. Get out of this town.* I wished I had my knife so I could make an incision and cut those words away. I ripped out the page and tore it into shreds.

Lord Jim was on my desk. I was supposed to write my final English essay. Show how the novel illustrates the themes of (a) man versus nature or (b) man versus man. I thought I'd fake learning for a while, in case my dad came into my room. I wasn't feeling very scholarly. *Lord Jim*—who gives a shit. I'd spent the whole year reading about the heroic adventures of Beowulf and Hamlet and Robert Plant. Swashbucklers and renegades—I'd had enough of their triumphs over life's obstacles. I threw *Lord Jim* against my bedroom wall.

When I went out into the kitchen, my father didn't even look at me.

Soup for dinner, big surprise. Seamus was the cook at Parsifal's, this health food restaurant that served seventeen kinds of soup. Heavenly Kale and Watercress, that kind of thing. The restaurant was always packed with scrawny college kids and stoned Dutch girls from the hostel. Thursdays, the poor could eat for free.

That night, the soup tasted scorched; black chard floated in the green.

On the serving bowl, porcelain roses were painted delicately. Everything in our house was secondhand, except for the pretty dishes. Everly's mother gave them to my parents as a wedding gift.

Legend has it that after the wedding my mother tried to smash all her heirlooms. Newly wed, they got high on acid in the honeymoon suite. My father tried to stop her, but she was tripping. Thought the cups were birds trying to fly.

She hurled china against the red-heart walls.

The broken pieces were beautiful, she said. The white shards looked like swans.

I've never met my grandmother; never seen a picture of her. Maybe she's arthritic and bald, senile in her Michigan mansion. My grandfather invented some kind of telescopic device, and when he died, he left his fortune to his wife and his only daughter, Everly. Everly was so generous. She gave all her money to the Pleasure Family.

If I became a model, would my grandmother recognize my face in a magazine? My dad said that lately I looked more and more like Everly; he said the resemblance scared him sometimes. She was sixteen when they fell in love.

First love is the hardest, my dad would say. Tears in his eyes.

First love is the most . . . Oh God, I couldn't take it when he got so weak. That's why I stopped asking about my mother. Just the look in his eyes, so lost at the mere memory, made me glad I'd never fallen in love and wasn't about to when I was surrounded by fools like Dean Black.

How was your day? my dad always asked me after school. But this time he didn't. Which was probably for the best. What would I say?

Dad, today I skipped school and met a man who told me I could make money as a model. His shrimpy friend begged me to come to his studio so he could shoot me. Test shots, that's what it's called, like you're the dummy on a firing range. These two men said they could help me move to New York and show up in the pages of *Seventeen*. My dad would be so disappointed if I told him I was tempted, even momentarily. He wanted me to believe that beauty was a bad thing. *Vanity led your mother down so many dark roads.* He cringed every time he caught me reading fashion magazines.

Why don't you read a book? he always said. Go for a walk on the beach? Darling, those magazines will kill your soul.

Dad, today I met a cool girl named China. She drank perfume and poured the pink water down between her bare breasts. She wanted me to go party at the King's Hotel. Hey, Dad, have you ever been to a party at the King's Hotel?

Hey, Dad, I said, real cheerful and nonchalant. How's business?

He didn't answer. Stood up, cleared his plate. I knew why he didn't want to look at me. Who could blame him? He would remember my ankles rising up in the air, my eyes closed, lips parted, letting out the long sigh.

I had to do something drastic to get the image out of his mind. Only, I couldn't think of anything to do. I stared at the roses, remembering how the slit in Justine's skirt tore when she ran away.

Finally, my dad spoke.

Did you ever keep in touch with any of those girls—from the—Oregon, you know, the—Family?

Why would I keep in touch with those girls? I hadn't seen them since I was eight. That's when we took off from the Pleasure Family. Three in the morning, leaving the commune, never saying good-bye. Pleasure is one thing, my father said, chaos is another.

Then we drove away in the Leader's van, switched the license plates in Portland, and drove in darkness toward Canada.

Even though Vietnam was long over, my father was still hiding from the FBI. So, after we made it over the border, my father made me promise to never, never, contact anybody in the Pleasure Family. Your mother is a traitor, he said, they're all traitors. You can't trust anybody, darling, even the people who were once your family.

Even if he hadn't warned me, I would never have wanted to keep in touch with the daughters. They used to call my dad Daddy. He was the only man who paid them any attention. Their real fathers were lolling around with my loving mother on the Leader's bed, or they were wandering naked down by the water looking for Pleasure in the Pacific.

Seamus never got into that sordid scene. He cooked pancakes for the girls. Daddy, they'd say, and they'd clutch on to his jeans, his flannel shirts. Sometimes I wondered what became of those girls, but most of the time, I really didn't want to know.

Why would I keep in touch with those freaks? You told me not to.

I just thought, if I needed to go away, you might want to have some friends around.

I have friends, I said, and then I stood up and started on the dishes. Always, I did the dishes. I kept our house clean. Paid the bills, did the laundry. I loved the safety of bank balances, the sharp smell of bleach.

You remember how I told you I was born with a fever? And that it returned for the first time around when I saw Justine? That's not quite true. There was one other time, but it's just not relevant to the case. Still, if I tell you, you might think my father less crazy.

The night we left my mother, we were just over the border when I started to burn. Sweat covered my body; my father said he touched my forehead and it was like putting his hand on coals. There were no hospitals, only highways and forests, and by the time we got to Canada, he was pretty sure I might die.

Tofino was pitch-black, pure forest, but somehow he found the ocean and doused me in the cold water. We slept without a tent, under the shade of the towering trees, and in the morning my fever was gone. He said I ran laughing across the beach, happy with the shells and sand castles, the seaweed and the abalone, happier than I'd ever been in Oregon. That was why he felt so grateful for the forests. He thought the trees saved my life. And I let him believe the myth. It probably made him feel less guilty about severing me from Everly.

Now my father fiddled with the straps of his overalls. I'd never seen him so tense and fidgety.

I stared at his dark brown eyes, the stubble on his cheeks. My dad's got the truest smile; people always trust him right away.

He took out his rolling papers.

Here we go. *Oh God.*

Sara, listen. You're so—this—just—you know—I—

He wasn't even high yet.

My father's problem is that he feels too much. Feeling fucks you up. You get hurt; you have to get high to stop the stress, the pain.

Don't care, I wanted to tell him. Just shrug your shoulders. Don't love your daughter so much. Don't be so moved by scenery.

I went and sat beside him. He used to braid my hair, and I was hoping he'd do it now, but he never did that anymore. Maybe he stopped when I turned sixteen; maybe he stopped because I looked too much like Everly.

He moved away from me.

He kept his eyes on the homegrown weed in his hands; he licked the seal. Rolling papers fell from his trembling hands.

He toked, talked about the house he would build in the forests with his hands. Solar panels, no electricity. He asked me when my last day of school was.

Twelve days, I said. I can hardly wait. I hate—

Look, darling, you—I—I've got to—to Eden. The moment is now. You can come up when you're done. That's what I think is best.

I can go with you now, I said, though I didn't want to go to the forests.

I'll get in trouble if I take you out of school.

No one cares. They don't even know I'm there.

Well, that nosy social worker knows. You raise your daughter alone, believe me, they're always watching you.

He rambled on about how the Trees in Eden were calling out to him.

Sylvia will come by and visit you, he said. She'll stay the night if you want.

No way, I told him. There is no way I'm living with Sylvia.

I feel—it's just that I'm not—you know. She can—I just can't—with you—you're at that age when a woman—

I am not living with fucking Sylvia!

I'd never sworn at my father before. He was crying, and now so was I. There was nowhere to hide.

I just called her. She won't live here. She'll just check up on you so you're not alone. She loves you, Sara.

She loves everybody. She loves a fucking blade of grass.

Please stop swearing. I can't stand what's happening to you.

Nothing's happening to me!

You used to— He didn't finish, but I knew what he was going to say.

I went and splashed some water on my face. When I turned back to him, he said, Come here. Let me braid your hair.

No, he didn't say that.

He said, I'm leaving now.

I could feel dampness on his skin, and I couldn't tell whose tears were falling onto my skin. I buried my face in the denim of his overalls. I held on to his small body with both of my hands. He tried to back away but I wouldn't let him.

Darling, he said. You used to be like me.

What he really meant: You used to be like me but since you're lying in the garden, loose-limbed and sighing, you're more like your mother, that nymphoheartbreakertraitor, Everly.

Steam clouds on the window. I watched him walk away.

I waved, but he didn't see. He climbed into the driver's seat of our old mud-streaked stolen van.

You probably think my father's to blame for all the trouble I got into. But I would never blame him for what ended up happening to me.

At least my father cared about something other than getting drunk or buying a Trans Am, which is more than you can say about most people in Victoria. And besides, girls my age were always getting by. In Africa, weren't girls my age rulers of their tribes? In New York, weren't they models with their own busy careers? In Victoria, weren't they managers at McDonald's? Whatever, lots of girls my age were getting by.

I thought maybe I should have a big house party like all the Mount Drug kids do when their parents go away on holiday.

Maybe I'd invite Heather and China here, and we'd have a big sleepover. Heather would whisper about the burnouts. China would scream about the sailor. And I'd tell them about my lover in the garden. My lover, the dirt.

Except, at that moment, I didn't really feel like seeing China or Heather ever again.

I sat on the floor, smashing my head between my knees. There I was in my still, fatherless home.

The fridge hummed.

THE ACE OF SPADES

I HEARD one voice saying, *I'm sixteen, I can't handle this,* and I heard another voice screaming, *Let's fucking party!*

The real voice was China's.

I'd come down here only ten minutes after my father left me. Early evening, and we were in her sometimes room on the second floor of the King's Hotel, lying on her single bed, listening to Motörhead. Both of us on our stomachs, facing a small window that looked out over the alley below. While I was worried and still, China was pretty much out of control.

After the sailor left her, she bleached her hair. Flinging her head in circles, her hair whipped, a white whirl. Dressed like she didn't give a damn, she wore a spangly tube top, tight gym shorts, and white sports socks pulled up to her bruised knees. Swigging Bacardi, she turned up the volume. Lemmy's voice blared from her small black boombox. His voice was husky and heavy as he sang over the bashing drums.

That's the way I like it baby. I don't want to live forever.

Heavy metal's never really been my thing. I like it a little more than Led Zeppelin, but it still makes me think of motorcycles and the brawny men in black leather who used to come to the commune and beat up my father.

But China loved the Ace of Spades.

And the song seemed to belong in her hotel room with the broken Bacardi bottles, the black lace curtains, the one-eyed teddy bear. She stood up on the bed and her hips swayed.

If you like to gamble, I'll tell you how you learn . . .

I had a dim idea that I should go outside and look for Justine, but I gave it up because I was here now.

Here now, in the King's Hotel, where I'd made a vow. *Promise me you'll do it. Yes I will Do It. Yes I will. I will.*

Outside, it had started to rain, and the night rain made the sky seem hopeful and diamondlike. Me and China, we were almost ready to Do It. I rested my head in my hands and tried to get a better look at the pale sliver of moon.

Stop looking so dreamy, China said. Standing above me, she raised her fist in a rock star way, as if she was onstage above a crowd of devotees all flicking their Bic lighter flames. Stop looking so dreamy, China said.

Let's fucking party!

We snorted cocaine off the cover of *Go Ask Alice*. China said Alice was her real name, but Alice doesn't live here anymore. So don't ask Alice, she said, and she threw the book against the wall.

Her dad made the whole book up, I said. That's what I heard. It's not even her real diary.

Doesn't surprise me, she said, doesn't surprise me at all. I like the other one better. It's more true. You know, she said, wiping her nose, the one with the tea party and the tunnels and Eat Me. Yeah, man, I like that one. It's more true. My mom named me after the girl in that fairy tale.

Since I'd arrived, cabbing it down here with the money my father left me for food, China had been confessing to me like a madman.

Maybe it was because I showed up in a beige raincoat which once belonged to Everly. I couldn't handle wearing my father's flannel shirts, and besides, I was tired of looking like an unsexy hick. Since I didn't have leather pants or a fur coat, I thought I should at least try to look elegant. My mother's trench coat was plaid inside, and the words on the worn-out label were London Fog. I don't know why Seamus held on to her coat because he generally tried to erase Everly as if she was a wife of chalk. China said the coat made me look like a private detective.

Maybe that's why she kept confessing.

She told me a lot of things which aren't really anybody's business, and I would never repeat them, but they were enough to make me hate the world. The world is just a fucked-up place. I really hated the world.

You've probably figured out that what Braun said about her was true.

Big surprise.

It was to me.

When she told me that she was what he said she was, I'd shivered as if the rain was suddenly falling inside of me.

The whole room looked different to me.

It was like when you get your eyes checked and they slide those magnifying glasses right in front of your eyes. Some things blur, some things are so clear you can't even see.

I saw the smashed bottles, the slash in her sheets, the place on the wall where she'd scrawled, No one here gets out alive.

But I didn't let on; I hid my surprise. The last thing I wanted was for a friend of Justine's to think I was naive. It was funny, though, because right after she confessed, she asked me if I would help her with this man. Please, she said, I need your help. So I can get out of here and go to Penticton. I'm ready to get clean. My mother's there. I think she's still alive.

How could I say no?

Especially because she'd also confessed that as soon as she saw me, she knew. I was the one. Other girls, she'd begged before, but they all said no way.

Even Justine, the girl you were asking about, I begged her and she said no way, and she's insane, man. But she wouldn't help me out. Not that she could have. She looks too fucked up.

So do I.

You? You look really clean.

I didn't feel like telling her that my face was a lie, that I only looked clean because I was cold and friendless and I pushed everyone away.

You're clean like a hospital, man. That's why I like you. Hospitals, I love. I've started OD'ing on purpose. I've OD'd five times just so I could go somewhere clean.

That got to me.

Another thing about China that got to me was this book called The World. She kept it hidden beneath her piles of dirty underwear. The World by Alice. Page after page of maps she'd painted from memory. Ivory Coast, Tunisia, Nepal. The paper was crumpled and sodden now, but her drawings of countries were still jagged and vivid. Her countries were surrounded by bright scarlet oceans and in her oceans there were black slit-eyed serpents and mermaids with hair like flames. She said she'd made *The World* when she was twelve, back in the days when she loved geography. I could memorize entire countries, she said, and draw them with my eyes closed. It was a kind of gift, that's what my teachers said. If you help me tonight, I'll be able to go to a school for drawing maps. They've got that kind of school, right?

Sure, I said, even though I'd never heard of such a thing.

Now I was part of her Plan, as fucked up as my dad's. We didn't need hammers and solar panels. We had to rely on her lips and her lies and mostly her hands.

Her hands. She took off her nail polish with Cutex Quick & Gentle. The paler the better, she said, though we'll have the lights low. My mother's coat thrown over the desk lamp so the light was a barely-there blue glow. She took off her charm bracelet because the silver heart and pony clanked against a roller skate when she moved her wrist. She stuck a toothbrush in her sock, and I thought of Justine, wondering if she'd done what we were about to do, but knowing even then that she never would. Neither should I, but I wanted to. Lose my innocence, which wasn't necessary at all.

A man upstairs banged on the floor, yelled in rapid-fire Chinese.

China ignored him, turning her music up as loud as she could.

You win some, you lose some, it's all the same to me . . .

I trusted her, even though she was coked up. Just kiss him, she said, make sure he closes his eyes.

Cocaine makes you feel invincible. Sure, man, I said, I'll kiss the Six Million Dollar Man. Bragging and tough, like I did this kind of thing all the time. Dean Black could hardly compare. He was my boyfriend; he was the one all the girls wanted to love. My former friend Tiffany Chamberlain tortured me when I started going into the bushes with Dean. I can't believe he likes her, she used to whisper so I could hear. She's not that pretty. She's weird. She used to live with those free-love freaks. Well, Tiffany could have Dean now. I was here.

I rifled through China's clothes, choosing a white flimsy dress, with a ruffle on the left side, a birthday party dress, the kind of pretty, frilly garment I'd dreamt of wearing when I was fourteen. China handed me her brown leather lace-up boots with heels three inches high. Witch boots, she said, that's what these kickass boots are called.

China backcombed my hair so it rose around my face like a wild red mane. She lent me lip gloss. It smelled like smoke and cherries.

You know I'm going to lose, and gambling's for fools,

But that's the way I like it baby. I don't want to live forever . . .

Lee Majors was about to arrive. That's what China called him. *The dude's loaded! He's the Six Million Dollar Man.*

The Chinese man upstairs yelled, Turn it down! China threw her bottle up at his voice and the bottle smashed against the ceiling, shards of glass falling down like lacerating rain.

*   *   *

Her bathroom was the smallest bathroom I'd ever been in. I sat on the toilet and my feet touched the wall. Blue mold on the tiles; dust of violet blush on the floor.

The shiver started in my back, seized me suddenly. My muscles started to contract as the chill coursed through me. My knees were bone white, goose-pimpled, and I went fetal.

My teeth were chattering and my jaw ached. The hair on my arms rose as I trembled. I might as well have been in a freezer. I tried to will it away, but I couldn't think of a warm place because I'd never been anywhere tropical. So I hugged myself, running my hands up and over my body as if I were my own comforter.

In the quiet of the bathroom, I heard my own voice again. I *can't handle this*. Get out, I told myself, you'll fuck this up. Just go home. Leave. I barely knew China; she might be setting me up in some perverted scam. I could go home, be consoled by Sylvia. In the morning, she'd bring me warm milk, thistle juice, let me miss school while I slept off the chill.

But I couldn't leave China in a room where men knocked on her door, never knowing, never caring, never asking about the maps she drew and saved. Call her what you want. Hooker, whore, slut, tease. She was the first girl to befriend me, and I would have done anything for her.

I *had* to Do It now. Lose the necessary innocence. And what good was it anyway? It was just like a library card or a set of spare keys, something small you lose and then realize you never really used. In the last five minutes before Lee Majors arrived, I envisioned innocence as a small trinket falling out of the King's Hotel and down onto the rainswept streets.

*   *   *

When I went back out, China was crouching on the floor smoking a cigarette, knees pressed against her naked breasts.

Hey, she screamed, so excitedly, as if I'd just entered the room for the first time.

Man, I said, lifting higher my wild mane, I'm a good kisser, man.

She smiled a little wickedly. That'll come in handy, she said. And then Lee Majors knocked on the door and I was the one who let him in.

THE SCHOOL FOR MAPS

THE Six Million Dollar Man turned out to be a dead ringer for my science teacher, Mr. Klein. Just last week, Mr. Klein told me I was wasting my potential dating a dumbass like Dean Black. Imagine what he'd think of me now. I'm sure he'd be disgusted, but Everly, she'd be proud. My mother idolized Patty Hearst. She kept Patty's photo on her mirror. The rebel heiress, the brainwashed hostage.

Yeah, Everly would be proud of me now.

Mr. Klein's twin brother sat nervously on the edge of the bed. His hair was orange and thinning; he wore wire-rimmed glasses; he crossed a leg over his knee. Like Mr. Klein, he was awkward, as if he'd never quite believed the length of his own overgrown body. Why would he want to be here? China, staggering around in her white sports socks, holding up two fingers in the headbanger's victory sign and looking like she might pass out at any moment. Me, standing near the bathroom door with my arms folded across my chest, glaring at him.

Well, hello, Tahiti, he said.

I didn't even know who he was talking about at first.

He had that fake way of laughing, like a lot of forty-year-old men. I guess they can't laugh naturally anymore so they just speak some words which vaguely resemble laughter. It drives me crazy, especially when they do it nervously, which is what he did when he looked at me. Well, hello, he said, har-har-har.

This is Fresno, China said, putting her arm around me.

I haven't seen you before, he said. He looked at me again, suspiciously, I suppose.

China winked at me, bit her lip; I'd never seen a girl so happy. Her skin was flushed and warm, and I thought, She's not the slightest bit worried. She's not scared at all.

I love redheads, he said.

Good for you, I thought, but I didn't say anything. I kept my eyes down, staring at the shards of glass shining in the shag rug.

She's shy, China rasped, still using her devil-like Lemmy voice.

I wasn't shy.

I really liked kissing. I could kiss Dean Black for hours, even though I wasn't in love at all. When I moved my hand as I lay in the dirt of our garden, I thought of French-kissing a man who touched me so lovingly. But now . . .

Wanting to imagine I was someone else, but I really couldn't think of anyone else who would do what we were about to do. Her words came back to me like a warning, too late. *I asked other girls and they all said no way.*

Behind him, on the bed, I climbed like some scarlet predator.

Lean back, I told the guy, close your eyes.

I knew I should sound seductive, but really, I couldn't. I sounded as sexy as a piece of wood. I'm surprised he didn't start to laugh. He just did what I told him, and I quickly leaned down to kiss him before he could change his mind and offer up his own idea of what I was supposed to do.

His lips were clammy and metallic. It was like licking a lock.

I thought he might complain of my cold skin, because his hand rested on my knee. But he didn't notice the chill that lingered in me.

With my head bent over his, it was hard to see China, but I glimpsed her from the corner of my eye. She was kneeling on the floor before him, as if she was about to pray. Her small hands fumbled with his belt buckle. She brought his jeans down. His pants seemed to swallow up her knees. I didn't glance at her lips, only at her hands. Her hands. Her hands moved to his pockets swiftly.

Then we were both racing.

I grabbed her coat and my bag, and followed her as she stepped out over the windowsill. The rails of the fire escape were wet, and I almost slipped as I climbed up the side of the King's Hotel, headed for the roof. China was far ahead of me, laughing and screaming, YesYesYes! I don't think she heard him, but I did.

I heard what he said.

When I was almost on the top step, I heard.

He must have come over to the window after he dressed. Maybe he yelled while his pants were still on the floor. Either way, I heard the guy. He might as well have had a megaphone.

You little red-haired bitch. I'll find you.

*   *   *

We ran. From the roof of the King's to another roof and another until we were at the end of Yates Street, and I could see the blue bridge rising up from the docks. The roof was low and flat; it was like standing on a long tar prairie.

I don't know why I'd never thought of going up there before. Maybe when I saw Justine, she was running toward a fire escape. As if she was reading my mind, China said:

All the Red Zoned girls come up here. The cops have no idea.

Then she spat on the tar. I spat too even though I had less of a reason to.

Fuck, that was hilarious, man.

Hilarious wasn't exactly the word I would have used to describe the Lee Majors episode.

You look so clean, man. He never suspected he was about to get rolled. Oh man, what an idiot. He thought he was in for a ménage à trois!

I guess she didn't realize that Lee Majors had threatened me, and I hadn't really gotten away with anything.

I felt very cold and scared and alone. I wanted to go home.

Hey, Sylvia, what's up? I just kissed a forty-year-old man while my hooker friend bent down on her bruised knees. Do you still love me now?

I'd never been threatened before. Being raised by a man like Seamus, I'd never so much as heard an insult. Call me sheltered, but his threat really frightened me. I kept hearing his hissing, hating, horrible, straight-to-hell words. *You little red-haired bitch. I'll find you.*

China was no help. She was pouring Love's Baby Soft on a T-shirt and wiping the sweet rag over her face to remove all her makeup. She looked so different when she was clean-faced. I saw her chapped lips, her raw, wary eyes.

Three hundred bucks, she declared. I told you that dude was loaded! That's enough for a scholarship, right?

Sure, I said, though I didn't have a clue how much a scholarship cost.

I didn't want any of his money. I told her to keep my share.

Visa, AmEx, MasterCard—I can sell these, China said. My uncle knows a biker who pays big bucks for plastic. I'm set for life. I'm gonna get my life together, you know. I am. No more hospitals. No more sucking—

I put my hands over my ears. I didn't want to hear those words.

Dude's name is Dirk Wallace! she screamed. Dirky!

She hurled his wallet down onto the street. I watched it twirl, like a fluttering fusillade.

The more she made fun of him, the worse I started to feel. Don't think I'm just saying that now, in retrospect. I really felt bad when she showed me the photo of his daughter, a dimpled, eager little girl. One of those Kmart Portrait Studio photos, the girl in pink posed against the background of a painted rainbow.

Dirk probably had the 4 × 6 on his mantelpiece. Sent the 3 × 3 to his mother.

On the back of the photo was written: Ashley, aged 6.

Good thing I'm getting out of here, China said. I heard about this one chick who rolled some family man and he ended up coming after her with brass knuckles. Fuck, man. You never know, right?

Yeah, sure. You never know, I thought.

Fucking Dirk Wallace, man. I don't give a shit about that guy. I don't feel guilty at all. Only thing I regret, man, is that I forgot my Motörhead tape. She licked powder from inside the pages of the *Go Ask Alice* paperback. I had never finished that book because I just knew she died at the end, and besides, I'd heard it was written by her dad. But even if it wasn't, why did girls have to always die at the end?

I opened the book to the last page, just to make sure.

Epilogue: The subject of this book died three weeks after her decision not to keep another diary. Was it an accidental overdose? A premeditated overdose? No one knows, and in some ways that question isn't important.

Wasn't important? Fuck off. How could they say that? The question was more important than anything.

China lay on my mother's coat and started to sing The Ace of Spades in this triumphant way, as if she was giving the fans her favorite farewell encore.

I walked over to the edge of the roof.

The suburbs were buried in darkness; so were the mountains and the wharf. You could see only the rain on the streets, lit up with streetlamps, and the now-and-then headlights blurred and red.

I decided right then that I wouldn't ask China about Justine again. I couldn't really tell you why. Ming, Ming, oh Ming. China was hard and careless, and she had her reasons, but Justine was different. She was careful and delicate in the way she stole and the way she sang. Justine would never sing Motörhead.

What's your problem? China said when I'd returned to her side. Why do you look so freaked out? Come on, man, you just pulled off a scam!

I didn't answer.

Do you think Justine's working? I asked suddenly.

Working? Justine doesn't work, man. She's too punk to work. Besides, I don't think she's even kissed a guy yet. Hey, what is wrong? I'd be dead without you. Think of that before you get all quiet on me.

She closed her eyes, my mother's coat draped over her like a morgue sheet.

Watch this, she said, her eyes still closed. She stabbed her cigarette out on Ashley's face. Red ember ground down, burning a blue hole in the little girl's eyes.

*   *   *

The roof was harder than a cliff, and I ended up spending the entire night just sitting cross-legged, staring at the pure black sky. All night, I didn't hear a siren or a scream or anything. I might as well have been in the forests with my father; it was just as still and quiet up above the sleeping retirement town. I kept thinking that I should go home before Sylvia discovered the note I'd left. *Hey Sylvia, Gone to Dean Black's for the week. Don't worry about me.*

I'd try not to think about Sylvia and then I'd just start thinking about Dirk Wallace. I kept seeing him awkwardly loping around his house in Oak Bay, trying to explain his missing wallet to his wife. His wife was probably named Sue. She was probably on to him by now. I want a divorce, she'd scream. Get out of here, you sleaze. Or maybe not. Maybe he'd just saunter into the police station and say he'd been rolled by two desperate girls in the alley behind the King's Hotel. Describe the assailant, please. Red-haired. Shivering. Skin like the Arctic Sea.

Across the way, I saw on a higher roof nearer Chinatown the shimmer of a girl.

Later, I'd find out the shimmer was Justine. She lay down on a rough roof, higher than mine. Like me, she pressed her back against pebbled tar. She held herself; she shivered and counted the stars.

*   *   *

Good morning, Fresno, China said, in a radio announcer's voice. It's a fine day in the lovely city of Victoria. We're expecting twenty-two inches of rain, and after these commercials, we'll bring you breaking news on the fine young daffodils Mrs. Smith has planted in her garden.

My stomach grumbled.

Let's go to the Get Laid, she said. It's on Dirk.

I was in no mood to see Stanley and his yellow teeth.

It is a delightful day, she said, holding my mother's jacket tentlike over her head to keep away the rain. Why are you so freaked out?

That guy threatened me. Last night.

You call that a threat? Man, I've heard way worse.

He sounded pretty angry, I insisted, because, believe me, he did.

OK, take this, she said, thrusting a gift into my hand. Lighten up, would you? Stop being so paranoid.

So that's how I ended up with the knife. The knife the cops are looking for, the knife they'll never find.

I probably shouldn't say this, considering, but I loved the knife right away. I might as well have been Sleeping Beauty, and the knife the kiss of a prince. My new knife was so much better than my corkscrew ensemble. Silver and smooth, the long blade shone. The blade was a skinny dagger, sharp and fine. I touched

it for a while, and then I flipped the blade back into the whatever it's called, the color of which, I think, is called opaline.

Take it, man, she insisted. Not that you need it, but you never
know, right?

Don't you want it?

I don't need it anymore. I'm leaving this shithole!

With that, she stood up and started ruffling my hair, tickling
me, doing her best to make me laugh.

Suddenly I realized she saw me as a little sister, a high school
girl. I wasn't the savior; she was the one who offered the real
comfort, the necessary help.

Keep my clothes too, she said. Keep the dress. Keep the fur.
Keep the boots. My shit suits you more than those stupid fucking long johns you were wearing yesterday.

Though I've never hugged another girl, I wanted to hug China.
How did she know that I'd wanted a new knife ever since I'd lost
mine? A knife like this, I never could have got on my own. It was
probably from a pawnshop, secondhand or—even better—contraband. I grinned at her as I slipped the knife into my boot. It
was too big for my bra. I could feel it, safe and solid, as we
walked over the roofs and reached the last building on Yates
Street. Pale gray smoke was churning out of a rising, immense silver chute. Behind the chute, there was a sleeping bag and a bottle
of shampoo. Hey, Athena, China screamed, her voice impatient
and almost furious. Hey, Natasha. There were no tears on her
clean face, but she really looked like she was going to cry.

Where is everybody? I kind of wanted to say good-bye.

When you walk toward the bus station, all of a sudden, you're
in fairy-tale land. Hit the tourist part of town, and you're on

cobblestone streets. Flowers and British flags bursting up all over the place. The pride of the town, the ancient Empress Hotel, is covered in ivy. Carriages drawn by white horses clop by. The streets smell like Earl Grey tea and horse manure.

Tourists love this shit, China said. Someone tell me why.

Myself, I could never understand the appeal of walking around a fake, old-fashioned British town. Supposedly, most tourists come from hectic, filthy cities and they're grateful for Victoria because it seems quaint and polite. Ye Olde England, that's what we're supposed to be.

We passed some idiot handing out pamphlets to the Wax Museum. She was dressed like Queen Victoria and China told her to fuck off.

It was fun, walking down there, with China. Two hungover girls, with tar in our hair and dirt in our mouths. Tourists threw us looks of disgust. Fuck you, China screamed to no one in particular, and we started smashing into tourists for no reason at all. I really wished she wasn't leaving because I could have watched her harass people for the rest of my life. Buddy, she screamed at this one befuddled character holding a crumpled map. Buddy, take our picture, please.

If you saw the Polaroid, you'd see how I was laughing, how we looked like lifelong friends. I kept the photo in my notebook as long as I could.

But it's gone now.

Guess where? It's with all the stuff the cops seized.

It's in the Evidence File, exhibit 13. You could check out the Polaroid, and probably never notice that I was holding the knife up like it was a middle finger. Cops noticed. They're saying I was "brandishing" the knife, but it was just a joke to freak out the tourist. How was I to know our careless photo would end up as evidence? I'm telling you now. Be careful if you ever take a Polaroid.

Anyway, if you look at the photo, you'll see what I mean about China being prettier than any of the smiling girls in stupid magazines.

Our bus station wasn't exactly glamorous. It's just one room with a couple of vending machines and maps on the wall showing our speck of an island surrounded by an endless blue ocean. DISCOVER CANADA, a sign said. I hated seeing our little island in the lowest place. I guess that was the point. You'd look at that skinny pathetic piece of land and want to buy a ticket immediately.

I watched China as she waited in the ticket line. From the back, in Everly's beige coat, she could pass for a private school girl. No one would ever guess that she was a girl who'd OD'd five times just so she could sleep somewhere clean. I watched her as she reached the ticket seller, startling the drab woman behind the grate when she yelled out, One way to Penticton, in her heavy-metal voice.

I guess it was the combination of starvation and a cocaine comedown because I started to cry and I had to cover my face with my hair when China sat down beside me. She wouldn't have noticed anyway because she was gazing down at the one-way ticket she'd bought with Dirk Wallace's salary.

Penticton, the ticket said. One Way. No Return.

I'm getting out of this shithole, she said for what seemed like the seventeenth time. I hope my mom's still alive.

I hung out with her for a while because I didn't really feel like going back to school yet. It was only 11:00. I had a feeling when I showed up there, tarred and furred, I was either going to get crucified or be treated like a rock star. One or the other, and I wasn't in that much of a rush to find out.

China rested her head on my shoulder as she smoked cigarettes and laughed about how she didn't feel guilty at all about Dirk Wallace, and how hilarious it would be if he went to the police station and told them to APB on Fresno and Tahiti.

Do you think he'll go to the police?

Oh, stop worrying about it, man. You didn't do anything.

She must have shown me the ticket five times.

The school for maps is going to be so cool, right, Sara?

Sure, I said. Penticton's a small town in a valley of vineyards and apple trees. I don't know if they have a school for maps there. Is there such a school at all? There has to be. With all my heart, I really, really hope there is.

ANOTHER STUPID
STONER SONG

IN the Mount Drug breezeway, I smoked cigarettes with some Grade Eight stoner-girls-in-training. You look cool, one girl said. Her braces spangled in the sun. Yeah, man, where'd you get that coat? I could have bragged, but I'd already decided to put the last twenty-four hours out of my mind. I couldn't go back to science class and study capillary action in geraniums if I was thinking about China on her knees and me kissing that man on his lips. I wanted to be a student for just a couple of hours, until I calmed down. My nerves were shot.

Unluckily for me, science class was canned. A pep rally in the auditorium to hype the crowd for the Rams' upcoming battle against the Oak Bay Oysters. Actually, that's not what they're called. Sorry but I forget the name of the enemy football team.

So I went into the gym, trying not to fall because the floor was waxy and my high heels were pretty high. I pulled dirty strands of matted hair down over my bloodshot eyes.

Meanwhile, Tiffany Chamberlain was straddling Vanessa Clark as the cheerleaders attempted a human triangle of purple and blue. One, two, three, four. Who do we adore? The Rams! The Rams! The Rams!

All I feel like telling you right now is that there was an "incident" at the back of the bleachers.

You can find the details in my file. I don't really feel like getting into it now.

*   *   *

After the "incident" I got called into the office and given a talk about my unseemly appearance and how I should consider anger management. My file was annotated.

No answer at Father's home. Mother's whereabouts unknown.

Eleven days till graduation. I decided to drop out of school.

At the rate I was going, I wouldn't ever get it together and have a career, so what difference did a diploma make? I didn't even care.

I went back into the bushes.

I went back to the bushes to find Heather Hale.

I sat down in the quiet clearing, resting my head against the moss on a damp rock. Gray clouds moved across the fading sun.

Anger management classes, what a joke. Mackie Hollander beat up skinny boys every day. He pushed them in lockers; he shoved their heads into toilets and flushed while they cried.

Hey, slut, he'd said to me as soon as I entered the pep rally. Hey, slut. Come here and show that sweet ass to Mackie.

Once you lose control, it's hard to stop.

Hand over the knife, Principal Dave Locke had ordered, or you're banned from school premises. It wasn't much of a bribe.

Now, I still had the knife with me, and when I heard boots breaking over fallen branches, I kept the knife ready in my hand.

Bryce looked pretty goofy, rocking his head to some imaginary song.

Hey, Ice Queen, he said, like everything was still the same.

I narrowed my eyes, gave him a dirty look. The long silver blade pointing like an arrow on a compass.

He didn't even notice my blade. He just sat down on the rock above me. He took out his little plastic baggie and rolled a spliff. There it was, the familiar smell of pot.

Raped any girls lately? I wanted to say, but I didn't.

I just stared at him, thrusting the knife in my hand, hoping he would get nervous and stutter. But he toked away, a slow, silly smile on his face as if he was trying to remember a good joke he'd heard yesterday. He'd grown a faint mustache; a rash of pimples reddened his chin. It was hard to imagine why I'd ever been nervous and quiet around him.

You look pretty agitated, he said. Drawling the word, *aaagitaated*. It sounded like some kind of surfer's move.

I slid the knife back into my boot. I could have been carrying a machete. Bryce was too high to notice anything beyond the fact that I wasn't smiling.

Where's Heather? I asked.

Don't know, don't care, he said.

He was sitting a few feet above me, and I lifted my hand. Teasingly, I pulled on the frayed cuffs of his blue jeans.

Hey, Bryce. I just stabbed Mackie Hollander.

Yeah, right, and I just fucked Nadia Comaneci.

When did he get such a dirty mouth?

You couldn't hurt anyone, he said. You're too shy.

Shy? I was a lot of things, but I wasn't shy. Just because I didn't talk to him, just because he was boring, just because he had nothing to say. His eyes were watery and red, and I suddenly wondered what he would be like when he was forty. Would he be like Dirk Wallace? Who would I choose to marry? Dirk or Bryce? Not that those were my choices, but I was losing my mind, starting to wonder about the strangest things.

You wanna get high? Bryce said. You're aaaagiitaated. I can tell.

Angry, agitated, call it what you want. The whole conversation with Mr. Locke, the principal, was bringing the fists back into me, I could feel them, a thousand fists pounding under taut skin.

Mr. Locke asked me to apologize to Mackie. He looked at me like I was contagious; he read my file and then gave me his lecture. His lecture went something like this:

Sara, it's understandable that you have some antisocial tendencies, considering that you lived in That Place. But now you have the choice to become part of Normal Society. If you want to continue your studies here at Mount Douglas, then you'll have to show a commitment to responsibility. I realize from Mr. Klein that you have been an attentive student and your boyfriend has been a bad influence. I'll speak to Dean as well.

I mumbled Fuck Off when he blamed it on Dean.

That's when he suggested the anger management classes. Held from 4:30 to 6:00 at the Boys and Girls Club.

Anger management—the phrase made me laugh. As if anger was something you could manage like a bank account or a small business. Put this fury here and let it earn some interest for seventy days. Yeah, fuck off.

I didn't pull the knife on Mackie because I'm angry, I said to

Principal Dave Locke, who, by the way, is known as Shaved Cock. I did it because *he's* really mean—

That was pretty much the end of my education, as soon as I said that.

*   *   *

Bryce was lounging, leaning back against a fallen log. He looked like the happiest guy alive. I could never have a serious conversation with him. I could never say, Tell me why you did that to Heather. How could you do that? Why would you do that?

Because he'd just smile, shrug his shoulders, and say, Don't know, don't care.

I felt the blade against my warm skin. I hadn't even showered since the whole rolling-Dirk-Wallace episode. Still, there was enough Love's Baby Soft on me that I could probably last for days before anyone noticed that I was incredibly unclean.

Where's Dean? Bryce asked, opening his eyes at last.

How should I know?

He's your man.

He's not my man. I dumped him.

That's what I said, even though I hadn't officially dumped him.

So *that's* why you're agitated. I get it now.

Before I could tell him I was agitated because he'd done something to make Heather disappear before my eyes, I heard the snapping sound of branches being broken as another burnout approached. Luckily, it wasn't Dean. Bruce was wearing a brand-new black leather coat; his mom had already sewn his old ZoSo suede patch on the back. Dean was always complaining about how spoiled Bruce was, how his mom bought him a subscription to *Playboy*, as if that was the ultimate gift.

Whoa, Bruce said when he saw me. Sexy mama!

Bruce was always talking that way. He watched too much TV.

I really didn't want him to think I was sexy. God knows what the burnouts would do if they found me sexy.

Sexy mama, Bruce said, bounding over, draping his arm around me. I heard you stabbed Mackie in the pep rally. Fucking hilarious, man! I wish I had that on tape!

I didn't exactly stab him. I just held the blade to his face.

Didn't know you had it in you, Sara. I'm impressed.

He ran over to Bryce, grabbed the joint, and the two of them tussled in the dirt.

Come on, Sara, Bryce said. Sit up here with us and get high.

I wanted to hate those guys, and it was pretty difficult, because all of a sudden they were being so nice to me.

I took the joint and sucked the smoke down, holding it in my throat until I could no longer breathe. I choked and coughed, and they didn't even laugh. Really, I wondered, why are they being so nice to me?

Fucking pep rally homo jock shit, Bryce said. Let's just skip out. Sara, you wanna come back to my place? Drink some shit mix.

Shit mix. That's what they called the stuff we drank after Bryce's dad grounded him for drinking from his bottles of alcohol. We'd started taking a little bit from each bottle and mixing all the liquor together. The burnouts could be surprisingly smart when it came to the eternal quest for booze.

No, I gotta go meet someone, I said. And I did. Besides, I knew if I didn't get out of the bushes soon, I'd end up back at Bryce's house, listening to Led Zeppelin. Next thing you know, I'd have drifted back into being the stoner girlfriend.

I stood up, brushing dirt off the back of my fur coat.

Hey, Bryce said, almost desperately, Dean got you a job. Did you hear about that?

No, I hadn't heard about that.

Yeah. He got you a cooking gig at the camp. He pulled some strings. It's good money too. Ten bucks an hour! We're leaving on Friday, he went on. June the fifth. Tell me now if you're coming 'cause otherwise I'm gonna give your space in my truck to Petey Pearce.

I didn't answer. Bruce rolled a new joint and passed it to me first. For a while, we sat there getting high and reminiscing about old times. Remember the time Bryce passed out at his grandmother's and Dean wrote 666 in shaving cream all across Bryce's chest? Remember this, remember that. It was like falling down into a drowning lake. They'd been my only friends, and where else was I supposed to go? If I went back downtown, I'd have to worry about Dirk Wallace wrecking my face with brass knuckles. I'd probably watch Justine run by me again, as if I was white air. Maybe I'd meet another girl who would enlist me in a crime and then take off to be with her family. I didn't know what to do. It probably doesn't seem like much of a problem to you but I really felt like I had nowhere to go. I'd been more or less kicked out of Mount Drug, so I didn't have anywhere to sit during the day. And I couldn't go home because Sylvia was probably waiting there with a birth control brochure and a cup of hot peppermint tea. I could go to that place Kool-Aid. It was some emergency shelter, probably run by Born Again Christians who would probably make me pray and give up my knife. Kool-Aid—I bet the guy who invented that name thought he was so clever and had no idea his name was incredibly corny. I knew if I walked in there and some Christian said Welcome to Kool-Aid, I'd start laughing and get kicked out before I'd even signed in. So forget that place. I wasn't going there.

Maybe I belonged in the forests.

I'd been raised in the cool shade of constant evergreens.

I'd swim, I'd suntan. I'd cook for loggers; I'd be their tanned gourmet. On my day off, one of the loggers could drive me to visit my father. He'd be overjoyed, seeing me in overalls. I'd help him break ground, just the way I used to when I was his little girl, his best friend.

You gonna come or not? Bryce asked.

Yeah, yeah, I said. I'll come. June the fifth.

June the fifth was two weeks away. I had plenty of time to find Justine.

Where's Heather? I said suddenly.

You didn't hear? Bruce said, and he started to laugh. He choked on smoke, and when he was finally able to breathe, he told me the news.

The Hole checked into Ledger Hotel.

It's not funny, Bryce said.

You thought it was pretty funny when I told you yesterday.

Yeah, well, now I don't.

I always knew that bitch was insane, Bruce said. She probably ran out of guys to fuck. I bet that's why she . . .

I wasn't listening anymore.

The Ledger Hotel, the Ledger Hotel.

Ledger was no hotel. You'd think the King's Hotel was the worst place for a girl my age to end up, but you'd be wrong. Ledger was down a long lane, and once me and the burnouts drove down there on Halloween. Driving down the long dark lane, where everything seemed so perfectly normal and serene.

Spooky, Dean had said. Let's get the fuck out of here.

I thought of Heather held in that haunted house. I thought I might start to cry.

Bryce passed me the new joint, but I just held the skinny spliff in my hand. Suddenly I noticed the stain of his saliva.

There was no way I was putting that thing in my mouth.

When I pulled the knife on Mackie, I'd felt a rush of adrenaline. Call me antisocial, but I'd rather have that feeling than the way I felt when I heard Heather was locked in Ledger. I couldn't stand feeling. Feeling fucks you up. I know it does.

You look freaked out, Bryce said.

I was getting sick of people telling me I looked freaked out.

She wasn't even your friend, Bruce said. So what do you care? She always told us she thought you were a snob.

Fuck off, Bruce. You guys are just teasing me, right? Heather's not in Ledger. Fuck off!

Man, when did you get so mouthy? Just smoke the doob, will you? That's prime weed.

Maybe they were right. Heather was a bitch. Insane. And her stint in Ledger had nothing to do with the garden hose, nothing to do with my ex-boyfriend, nothing to do with me in the bathroom, mumbling sorry and not telling her I hated those guys for what they did. Look at China—after all, China had been through much worse and she'd managed to get herself on a bus. Mr. Klein told us the theory the Church tried to ban. Survival of the fittest. Only the strong survive.

That's right, I thought, I know the theory's true.

I handed the joint to Bruce, brushed the dirt off my hands, and drew out my knife. I should have stabbed the both of them, but I just drew a little heart in the dirt. Don't ask me why. I drew a little black heart and then I kicked the dirt heart with the edge of my heel.

June fifth, Bryce said. I'll pick you up at your place. Pack lots of sweaters 'cause it gets real cold at night.

No shit, I said. I think I know.

Christ, chill out. I just don't want you catching pneumonia.

Hey, Sara, I got a job too, Bruce said proudly. Pumping gas at the Cadboro Bay Mohawk. I gotta wear one of those blue welfare suits and be a gas jockey for all the rich bitch Cadboro Bay biddies. But I don't care. I'm just gonna get super high every day.

Yeah, well, we're gonna get high up in Horsefly, Bryce said. I'm bringing my bong and we're gonna get high all day long.

Then he sang it like a song.

Gonna bring a bong, gonna get high all day long.

Bryce laughed, and Bruce laughed.

Gonna bring a bong, gonna get high all day long.

I laughed too, and that's why I hate weed. It makes you laugh at things that really aren't funny at all.

LYING AT LEDGER

THE cherry blossom trees were gifts from a Chinese emperor, that's what I heard. I thought they must be the most beautiful trees in the world, and it was a shame they were planted on the long lane leading to Ledger House. Delicate and black, the branches bloom with pale pink petals. When there's a breeze, the sky is full of a soft fluttering.

I reached over and sliced a slim branch. I thought I'd give it to Heather since I didn't have a Get Well card or a cheery bouquet.

I thought I'd ask for a room because I wasn't feeling so well myself.

Then, after a good night's sleep, I'd burst into Heather's room with all the energy of China. *Hey, man,* that's what I'd say, *let's party!* I'd break her out of the loony bin if I had to, smuggle her out in a laundry cart and bring her down to meet Justine.

As soon as I walked in through the front doors, I wished I had dressed more respectable. The place was very official and stern. A grim gray-haired woman in granny glasses banged away on a typewriter. Behind her, beige filing cabinets lined an entire wall. The whole place felt so beige and dead and serious that I wanted to scream.

Hey, I said to the tightass typist, where's Heather Hale? I want to see her right now!

I'm sorry, she said primly, our guests aren't allowed visitors.

Guests—I swear that's what she said. As if Ledger was some ritzy cocktail party instead of the place where cops put psychos and suicide attempts.

I sat down on the beige couch, holding the cherry blossom branch between my knees. She typed away, ignoring me.

Heather used to strut around school in her tight jeans and white pumps.

Now, she was probably sedated.

She was somewhere, somewhere in a silent room.

Heather, wake up, kick-start your heart, remember how you used to be a tough stoner girl. How you used to write AC/DC on your notebook, drawing the lightning bolt all jagged and fierce. Remember how the first time Dale called you Hole, you just turned very slowly and said, Dale, shut your fucking mouth. Don't you. Can't you. Remember how you drank from your flask of gin right in the middle of science class.

If only I could break through the beige door with the long steel bar, shake her, and say, Remember how tough you used to be. But what if I did break through, went up to her room and saw her comatose? Her blond wings might be shaved away, her scalp nicked with blood and yellow stubble. Her skin might be sallow and tinged with blue. A stiff white cloth might be covering her entire body, chafing under her chin. Or she might be perfectly calm, and look at me with blank, blind eyes. I thought that would be even worse. If all her toughness was gone, if they'd told her she needed to change. That would be the worst thing—if she tried to turn into a good girl because of what those idiots did. If I looked at her, and she just said, Sara, I'm all better now. I'm *so calm*.

I stood up and walked right over to the lady with a new plan. I thought I'd act a little crazy so they'd have to put me in a room. Once I took acid and I tried to remember how it felt to trip so I could start talking gibberish. There was a poster of that annoying Garfield cartoon, that stupid fat orange cat. What I thought I'd do was this: I'd point at Garfield and start ranting about how he was Jim Morrison. Giggling madly, I'd say, Hey! It's the Lizard King! Then I'd get on my hands and knees and start crawling across the floor, mumbling Riders on the Storm. Maybe I'd roll over on my back and start to drool.

China could have done it. She would have been so great, just flipping out and spitting all over the place. 'Cause she could lose control. And I just couldn't. It made no sense. A febrile heart, fissures in my veins, and still, I couldn't lose my cool.

So instead, I just placed the wilting blossom on the small beige wall separating me from the typing lady. How's Heather doing? I said. Is she OK? I tried my best to sound friendly so she'd be on my side.

All patient information is confidential, she said. She sounded just like a robot. Like R2-D2.

Can you just tell me if she's alive?

But no, she said no. No, I cannot tell you anything.

I pleaded with her for a while, saying Heather was my good friend, I just wanted to know if she was alive. For fuck's sake, I almost said, stop typing and just nod your head. Tell me she's OK. Because she shouldn't be in here; she should be running around on the roofs downtown. That's where she should be.

I took out my notebook and drew a map. I put Ming's on the map, and above Ming's, I drew a lightning bolt. Then I made a line for Yates Street, and where the alley was, I drew a little crooked star. Heather, I wrote, come and meet me here and we'll have a good time. Love, your friend, Sara.

I tore the page out of my notebook and handed it to the robot. I turned my back on her before she had a chance to tell me that guests weren't allowed correspondence.

As I walked back down the lane, pink blossoms were still fluttering through the air, and when I lifted my head I saw a single white seagull soar up from the gray wet rocks of Arbutus Cove. And me, just running down the lane because I didn't want to think about Heather anymore, and the blossoms and the bird seemed so wrong, like I didn't deserve to see all that. All that beauty.

ACROBAT

In the alley where I last saw Justine, there was no sun. The storefronts displayed carnation bouquets and orthopedic shoes and hearing aids, but in the alley, these same stores were just dark walls, and looking at them was like looking at the back of someone who has turned and walked away from you. I found a fire escape and walked up the steel stairs quickly, as if I was being followed. I swear, I could still hear his threat. I'll find you.

I sat on the roof and thought, This will be my bed for the night. How could I complain? Knowing Heather was in Ledger, I would never complain.

I flirted with ideas. A holdup, a hostage-taking, a getaway. I could point my knife at the neck of a pilot and scream, Take me to New York. But I didn't know where the airport was. I could steal a car, but I didn't know how to drive. I was so pathetic it wasn't even funny.

Right then, my father was building his new house. I thought of him surrounded by his beloved trees, drinking black coffee while he whistled a Neil Young song. He was probably running his hands through Sylvia's hair and she was smiling up at him patiently.

And China, she was probably in Penticton by now. I wished I could call her but I didn't know her last name. Penticton should hold a Welcome Home parade for China. They should hoist her up on the roof of a souped-up Cadillac and cover her with confetti. Hail the conquering hero. Why not? They always had those parades for men who'd fought in wars.

I couldn't keep my thoughts straight, and I wasn't even high.

Raising my head, I saw the sky caught halfway between black and blue. The American mountains, rising from the fading fog, looked just like a faint, jagged white wall.

End-of-day traffic started up in the streets; rows of cars heading back to suburbia. I bet Dirk wasn't driving anymore because his license was gone. He was probably pacing Yates Street with brass knuckles and a brawny buddy he'd recruited from the bar at the King's Hotel. Maybe he was with those two burly loggers who had talked about putting Justine over their knee.

Little red-haired bitch, she owes me. She owes me big time. I'll smash her slutty face. I'll do damage to her, damn right. I'll make her pay.

When I was sitting alone on the roof, all the things I'd noticed about Justine suddenly made sense.

I understood why she hacked and dyed her hair. I understood the toothbrush around her neck, the way she'd rushed down the streets.

You little red-haired bitch. I'll find you.

I ran my hands through my hair, and it was worse than Medusa's, but still not enough of a disguise.

I decided I'd steal some scissors and cut my hair and tear my skirt. That way I wouldn't have to hide up here for the rest of my life. I'd find Justine now, and this time I wouldn't be afraid. Because I understood her in a way I hadn't before. I understood everything, even Ming's advice. *Everyone hates you. Stay off the streets.*

She hadn't stayed off the streets, and I wasn't going to either. I knew that I'd committed a crime and Dirk could beat me up or tell the cops to throw me in jail. I didn't really care.

China said juvie was fun.

Inside, she called it. Standing on her bed, belting back Bacardi and dancing, she'd just laughed about how they called her crime *solicitation for the purposes of.* Big words for a little girl, she said, ha, ha, ha. Waving the bottle in the air like a sword. Juvie is summer camp, man. The food's good, all my friends are in there. It's like high school without the cheerleaders and the bops. That's what China said about jail.

I had this sudden urge to punch someone in the face.

*   *   *

I wandered over to the bus stop on Yates Street, and every old lady seemed to shoot me a worried look of grandmotherly concern. Sweetie, one said as I leaned my burning body against the plate-glass window of the hearing-aid shop, are you lost?

I ran away from her and went into Merle Norman. That's the pink makeup place; they give girls free samples and charts showing you how to make over your face. I felt so dirty, I thought I'd scam some cold cream cleanser.

I looked in the mirror and I looked really fucked up.

The saleslady in pink, she started getting tense, saying, Can I help you, can I help you, as I rubbed red lipstick on my eyelids and blue eyeshadow on my lips.

If you're not going to purchase anything, I'm going to have to ask you to leave.

*   *   *

I was aloft, a derelict acrobat. I climbed up fire escapes, hoisting myself over ledges, jumping over gaps. Hours, I searched. I walked through alleys, carefully casting my eyes in corners where weeds grew from concrete.

The runaway clues, I returned to. On the roof where China had taken me, I found Athena's sleeping bag.

China had told me all about Athena, a bank robber she'd met in juvie. A fifteen-year-old girl who'd held up the Royal Bank at the corner of Yates and Douglas.

Athena's sleeping bag smelled like rain and smoke. A pink plastic barrette was on the plaid cloth, a few blond hairs in the silver clasp. The shampoo bottle was gone, replaced by the newspaper. I glanced through it to see if there was news of our crime. FRESNO AND TAHITI ON THE LOOSE. Of course there wasn't. On the front page, it said TWO KAYAKERS FEARED DEAD.

China was right. *Where was everyone?* Maybe Dirk figured out that we ran up to the roofs. Maybe there'd been a sweep. Victoria wouldn't want bank robbers and hookers running rampant when all the tourists were starting to arrive for their vacation in the City of Gardens, God's country.

I decided to take a nap. I was pretty tired, actually, and I couldn't come up with a smarter plan. I lay on my side, holding my knees against my chest. I took off my coat, and the white fur was no longer soft, no longer white. It was gray and gritty, as if it had been rinsed in rain. In the slits of the pockets, I felt for cocaine and found only a fading sweet smell. I closed my eyes. It was a good thing the fever was under my skin 'cause I didn't wake up even when the night sky let down a light black rain.

I might have slept all night except the sky was too dark and I was scared and I just wanted to go down again. I had a sudden craving for a milk shake. Ming's, I thought, I'll walk in there, and say, really casually, Hey, Ming, where's Justine? He seemed like a nice guy. He'd probably give me her new address.

Only when I climbed down from the final roof, I wasn't near Chinatown at all. I didn't have a fucking clue where I was. Warehouses rose up off sloping hills and railroad tracks lay like black iron welts in the wet grass.

I crossed the street so I was closer to the water's edge.

That's when I saw her.

A skinny girl, knock-kneed and slanting, as if she was being drawn down by the weight of the suitcase in her left hand. She wore a man's blazer and the same torn skirt. Suddenly I realized that we were exchanging a smile. There wasn't anything welcoming about her smile: it was just a quick flicker of recognition.

I stopped and faced her. She stopped too and tilted her head, smiling. But what could I say? What should I do?

Justine, I finally said, in a wan and timid voice.

It was too late; she had already turned away. She headed down a slope I'd never noticed before. The hill led down to the docks and it was ragged with reeds. By the time I'd crossed the street, she was gone. The water down there was black and smelled like gasoline.

Reeds scratched across my face as I stumbled back up the hill, slipping in the damp mud.

When I was on the street, I looked around me but saw no one at all. A streetlight turned on and the black water shone.

*   *   *

Le Gardin: I swear that's what the place was called. Spelled incorrectly, that's not my mistake. I went in there, thinking it would be a seed factory, and instead it turned out to be this brand-new fancy restaurant with chandeliers. I managed to sneak by the poncy man in a tuxedo who was folding white napkins into birds.

In the immaculate bathroom, I drank cold water straight from the faucet.

There were no customers in Le Gardin, so I thought no one would care if I crashed on the bathroom floor. I wasn't feeling so great. It felt as if flames were burning a long line up through my spine. I needed sleep. I hadn't slept in two days. I hadn't eaten since my father's last meal. No wonder I was getting all delusional. She was a mirage, I was sure. You know how desert heat makes wanderers imagine an oasis? The skinny girl was my mirage, a vision from this heat.

I turned the tap on so the water would overflow and cover me as I slept.

The water poured over the edge of the porcelain sink. The cold water kept spilling down and I let it fall. The cold water flowed over me, covered me completely, covering my burning face and body.

I fell asleep in my man-made lake. Maybe I fainted or maybe I passed out or maybe I just hit the skids. Who cares.

The tuxedo man cared. He came barging in. What is going on? he said. He stepped over me and turned off the tap. There's a flood, he screamed in this high-pitched squeal. Do you hear me? My God, we can't have a flood!

I told him I was just having a nap, and I kept my eyes closed. I liked the floating feeling. There must have been seventy inches of water washing over me.

I tried to convince him, to will him away, but he kept saying I didn't look well at all.

You don't look well, he kept saying, and I fainted when he tried to hold me in his arms.

I'm sure he was trying to help when he called the Street Outreach worker, some gangly guy with Bible breath. At the time, I thought I must have had a high temperature. Drenched from head to toe, I was still burning; I must have hit 110. But later, I'd find out it's the smallest things that can get you put in White Oaks.

It's letting the water overflow on the opening night of a fancy place called Le Gardin. It's the toothbrush in the pocket, the pink barrette. The smell of rain and smoke. It's the runaway clues. It's when you won't give them your father's whereabouts. It's when they ask you where your mother is and you say somewhere in California and you start to cry.

THE RED ROOM
AT WHITE OAKS

AT White Oaks, they gave me quizzes. *How do you feel about your-self? How would you describe your physical appearance?* I'm fragile and pale, I wrote, my eyes are clear blue. Really: I'm strong, my eyes are green. All the quizzes they give girls. Amber, my room-mate, brought me faded issues of *Seventeen*. Their little quizzes: "Ten Flaws and How to Fix Them." How to make your narrow eyes wide and your wide eyes narrow. How to slim your hips and hip your slims. Fuck that, I threw the magazines at Amber and told her to go away.

* * *

My first night at White Oaks, I slept like an old man on his way to death. I dreamt a whole opera. Though I've never seen an opera, in my dream I knew exactly how it would be. A Viking woman; a hunted man. Blood of the lamb; a white-haired child washing himself with the green sea.

*   *   *

I ignored Amber because she read *Seventeen*. She wanted to do a makeover on me. Showed me the Before and After page. After, the girls smiled; they looked stupid and saved. Amber did everything *Seventeen* told her to do. Cucumbers on her eyes, lemon juice in her hair. She had a very round face, and her skin was so shiny. I've never seen a girl with such shiny skin. I think she wanted to look more exotic because she tweezed her eyebrows till they were thin black arches and she always wore this incredibly dark, violet lipstick. I'm making her sound freakish, but she was really beautiful and she didn't seem disturbed at all. She was taller than me, taller than Dirk Wallace, but unlike him, she didn't seem at all awkward with the length of her body. I don't know why, but whenever I'd look at Amber, all determined and long-legged, I'd imagine her climbing out of a car wreck while the slow, sluggish passengers burned inside.

After I told her to go away, Amber wouldn't leave me alone.

Then I found out she was the B & E queen.

Sometimes she needed a crowbar; other times all it took was a dime. Once, she turned a combination lock with her tongue. It was funny because she didn't even want to steal. All she wanted to do was get inside. In April, she broke into every locker at Oak Bay High School. By May, she was hitting mansions in Uplands. Last week, she'd been busted after she broke into eight offices at some insurance place.

I'm not going to stop, she told the judge.

Why not?

Because I'm good at it, you dickhead.

I'm skilled, I've got the gift. I'm a motherfucking Houdini!

The judge didn't want to send her to juvie. She thought Amber would enjoy being in a place with thirty-two locked doors. So they put her in White Oaks, the temporary shelter for troubled girls, and that's how she ended up sharing a room with me.

I told Amber I'd let her do a makeover if she taught me how to break and enter.

Just the basics, I said, I don't need anything fancy.

My gift is not a basic, she said. And besides, Sara, you just got here. You ain't ready to escape.

*   *   *

I fell asleep during a rerun of Charlie's Angels. I remember Charlie's voice. Girls argued over Bosley: Isn't that the guy from Happy Days? No, that's the Garbage Bag Man.

Jill, Kelly, and Sabrina were all gathered around a desk and his voice came out of a box and told them to put on bikinis and infiltrate the millionaire's pool party. Oh, Charlie, they giggled. They did what he told them to do even though his voice had no body and he never appeared in their room. My opera, he wasn't in it, though I fell asleep to his voice.

*   *   *

Amber said in my sleep, I turned to her and said: Enemy.

Oh, I'm so sorry.

No, it was cool. Sara, I wanna French-braid your hair.

I don't want a makeover, Amber.

I'm Houdini, I'll make you reappear.

You don't have barrettes.

I'll find a way.

At White Oaks, the other girls whined to their journals. They scrawled lipstick distress signals on the bathroom wall. *I'm so loveless, I'm destroyed, Oh God help me, I'm screwed.* But Amber said, *I'll find a way.*

So I let her braid my hair. She twisted my bangs, left the rest of my hair alone. The braid was lopsided and stiff, sticking out above my forehead like a unicorn's horn. The girl on the How to French Braid Your Hair page mocked me; her braid was like a perfect crown. But I looked better. It suits you, Amber said, lookin all wicked and deranged.

Later, we signed out for a smoke break. White Oaks is an old mansion, high up in a private forest. They don't need security because no one wants to leave. We sat on the porch, talking under our breath.

Don't let them put you in a foster home, Amber whispered. Say you have violent urges. Sara, I don't want you to leave. Promise me you'll stay here.

*   *   *

The art teacher couldn't keep his eyes off Amber. We were air-brushing rainbows when I overheard.

No, he said, don't make me do it again. I got in trouble last time. You shouldn't do that anymore.

Don't you get it? she said, gold spray paint on her palms. I'm Houdini. I can do whatever I want.

I used charcoal, drawing a girl running down an alley, smudging her legs till my fingers were black. I pretended not to overhear, but I had known for a while. Amber was up to something. She'd left our room at night, taking the barrettes I had found for her. I found them in the shower's drain. Good one, she said. You're almost ready to learn.

*   *   *

Cassie came down from the reservation for a six-week stint. They said she was *uncontrollable* because she threw a Johnnie Walker bottle at some guy.

She was barely five feet two with a vicious sneer. I liked her right away. The four other girls at White Oaks wore sweatshirts and jeans. Coke, Adidas, Mickey Mouse. But Cassie wore a suede jacket and ripped fishnets. Her hair was shaved short, except for a fringe of shiny black bangs above her dark eyes.

I'm a skinhead, she said, kicking me with her Doc Martens. Do you know what that is?

You're Pocahontas, some girl said. She slapped her palm against her lips. Owa-owa-owa. You've got fetal alcohol syndrome. You're a squaw.

Oh, you're really original, Cassie said, stomping across the rec room floor. Like I've never heard that before.

I wondered why *Seventeen* never wrote about skinheads. Why didn't they ever give advice on how to break and enter? I wondered why every girl in Victoria kept reading those magazines when they didn't offer one practical thing.

Cassie kicked the Angels. The TV toppled, fell off the stand. Cassie climbed on the TV. Die, she screamed. Die, Farrah, die!

*   *   *

The woman who ran White Oaks drove around in a silver Mercedes-Benz. She got money from Social Services to keep us off the streets. It's a kind of charity, I guess. Her office was full of awards.

I was brought there to discuss my fate.

They're a nice family, the Mickelsons. Sara, we think you'd

make more progress if you were out of White Oaks. You'd blossom with a nice family.

I like it here.

Well, the Mercedes-Benz lady said, playing with a gold pen, I'm glad to hear that. But we're a temporary shelter. And we only have space for girls who are suffering from severe trauma.

No offense, but I don't think a foster home is a good idea, I said.

Why not?

I've got violent tendencies. Violent urges. Violent dreams.

In case she didn't hear me, I said it again louder, like a chant. *Violent tendencies. Violent urges. Violent dreams.*

*   *   *

Amber used a nail the art teacher had given her. She showed me how to wedge the point to the left. We broke into Cassie's room. Three in the morning, we were going to the Red Room. The Red Room, I could hardly wait.

We ran up the stairs. Cassie did her best not to stomp.

Amber picked the lock with a barrette. The security in this place really sucks, she said. That was just way too easy.

The Red Room is where you go to calm down. The walls are padded; infrared lights sweep over you. These red lights were supposed to be a cure for anger. They were supposed to make us less uncontrollable, whatever that meant.

Cassie reclined on the floor. Red light swept over her furious face.

Amber danced around, flinging her body into the padded walls.

Sara looks like a narc, Cassie said.

She knows Justine, Amber said.

Oh yeah? Cassie said. Do you know where she's been hiding?

My face would give me away; I looked at the padded walls. The cushions were covered with a thousand footprints.

She's not gonna narc, Cas. Leave her alone. Remember China? That girl you met in the hospital? Sara helped her roll a john.

Cassie shrugged her shoulders as if to say, Big deal.

Amber ran to the door with a ripped page from *Seventeen*. The page covered the glass pane on the Red Room door. Stay Free, the Tampax ad said, and the girl on the bicycle was dressed entirely in white.

Under the red lights, I waited to feel calm, but I didn't feel any different.

Amber did it first. She showed me her scars. They started on her wrists and ended on her shoulders. Some of the scars were redder than the light of the room. The older ones were faded, raised lines like slivers of ivory. She took off her bra. There, above the nipple on her small breast, was a star with five points. It was so perfect and red, it might have been engraved in wood; it seemed impossible that the star was actually carved into her skin.

Who did that to you? I was going to ask, but I thought of Heather. Washing the dirt off her white pumps. *They wanted to do it so I let them.*

I looked away, but there was nowhere to look.

Cassie reached down into her underwear. Something glimmered in the dark V of hair. I looked away, but there was nowhere to look.

The glimmer was a razor blade.

Holding the small razor as if it was silk, Cassie carefully dragged the blade against the inside of her thigh. Blood trickled down. She smeared it across her knee. She didn't shout. She didn't scream. She just smiled as if she'd been lovingly touched by the kindest man. Could I do it?

Yeah, I could. I had violent tendencies.

Give me that razor blade, I wanted to say, but the words didn't come.

Give me that razor blade, Amber said. Cassie passed the blade to her. The blade was pressed between her thumb and forefinger. It might as well have been a joint.

Amber stroked the inside of her thigh, moving her hand closer to her underwear. She didn't take a big breath. She didn't close her eyes or anything. She just slashed. Amber slashed, slashing the blade in a long, straight line from the fullest part of her thigh straight to the white cloth of her underwear.

Oh God, she said, and her eyes closed. She let out a soft sigh.

Then I asked what I didn't want to ask. *Why?*

It feels really good. It feels like sex, Amber said.

It's better than sex, Cassie said. It's better than sex with gross, fat men.

I thought you had violent tendencies, Amber said.

I do.

Well, this will help you. Trust me.

I couldn't tell her that I was starting to get attached to my violent tendencies. They were better than my fever; I wasn't looking for a cure.

Cassie told me she was writing a book. Did I want to see it?

Not really, I didn't.

Show her page one, Amber insisted.

Page one, Cassie said, and Amber made a drumroll sound.

Page one, Cassie said, in the story of my life. Pointing at a place just below her knee, she showed me the letters. Tiny, but perfectly even. SLUT, the letters said.

Page two, she said, now pointing to the smooth skin under her arm. Here too the letters were so perfect and careful that I knew it must have taken hours for her to draw the word, hours when she couldn't have cried or shaken or asked for help.

BAD, the letters said.

Page three was written on her breast. She was only fourteen, so she didn't even have breasts. There was just a small rise of skin, a tiny nipple surrounded by pale pink, and three letters messier than all the others. FTW.

You don't know what that means? Cassie said. Justine has it too. On her wrist.

Oh yeah, I said, as if I was just remembering.

Fuck the World, Cassie said.

I've got it too, Amber said. It's down here. Look.

I just looked up at the surveillance camera. The lens was still and unmoving. A broken, useless eye.

You want it? Cassie said. You don't really deserve it.

She does. She helped China. She's tougher than she looks.

Fuck the World. I'd thought those words so many times they were almost part of my memory.

Yes, I said, and Cassie grabbed my hand. She wanted to do it on my shoulder, the place where I was once given a flu shot.

Expertlike, she cut in my skin with her small hands and smaller blade. I felt a dull, stabbing pain.

Feels good, doesn't it? Amber said, and she held my hand.

It didn't feel good though.

When I told her to stop, Cassie jabbed me with the blade.

You're a wimp, Cassie said. I've burned. I did it in juvie. Athena smuggled a lighter into her Tampax box. We burned flowers.

She showed me the small welt on her other breast. It might have been a poppy, a tulip; the skin swelled full and flowerlike. Her breasts were as small as those of a girl I used to baby-sit.

Annie Sanders; she was twelve. I'd read her *Anne of Green Gables* five hundred times. I suddenly thought I should call Annie's parents and tell them to get her out of Victoria before it was too late.

I want a flower, Amber said. Cassie leaned over and cut into Amber's breast. The two of them seemed to have gone into a trance, mesmerized by the damage. I waited for Amber to scream, but she smiled. Oh God, she said again, and she let out another sigh.

I felt a kind of envy. I left them there with the red lights weeping over their calmed bodies.

*   *   *

In Life Skills class, I tried to forget.

Today, the teacher said, we'll be talking about Breaking Barriers. We'll be talking about developing strategies for identifying and working toward Lifetime Goals.

Lifetime goals, what a joke. Maybe White Oaks should have a lifetime goal of fixing its surveillance camera.

Our teacher wore a pin-striped suit with a navy blue tie. Amber called her Gloria Steinem.

Gloria handed me a quiz. I'd probably filled out fifteen quizzes since I'd arrived at White Oaks, and each one seemed a little stupider than the one before.

This quiz had the usual multiple-choice questions. Choosing A, B, C, or D seemed a pretty careless way to choose a career.

In the '50s, Gloria said, women could only be wives and mothers. But now it's the '80s and you girls are *so* lucky. You can do *anything* you want.

Yeah, we can hook or strip.

What did you say, Amber?

I said I'm really looking forward to becoming an astronaut.

Normally, I deliberately fucked up my multiple-choice quizzes. I'd never check off my real choice. But for some reason that day I decided to be honest.

You witness a truck running over a rabbit. Would you rather
a. Write a story about the traumatic experience
b. Help a veterinarian treat the rabbit's injuries
c. Organize better road safety to prevent future accidents
d. Write down the license plate number of the truck and contact the correct authorities

I checked off b.

Cassie wrote FTW all over her form. SKINHEADS RULE, she wrote. OI!

Amber wrote NYMPHO as her answer to the question: What are your career goals?

We watched a video as Gloria marked our questionnaires.

This anorexic man was standing in front of an ugly gray concrete building. Bob T. Johnson, Ph.D., Oregon State University. When you identify your faults, you take the first exciting step in the process known as Change. I swear that's what he said.

Dude, Amber screamed, you need to eat some dinner.

I need some Change, Cassie wailed. Hey, Gloria, can you spare some Change?

Amber tried to read my answers, but I covered them with my hand.

After Life Skills class, Amber told me she wanted to break into Brandy's room and steal her Maybelline. I told her I'd catch up with her later. I've got to talk to the doctor about my temperature, I said, which was true. I'd spent the night in a suffocating sweat.

After class, I lingered near the overhead projector. I don't know why I cared. I slouched toward Gloria, asking her for my results.

Well, Gloria said, adjusting her glasses and surveying my form. You show an aptitude for the helping professions—nursing or veterinary medicine. Would you like to talk more about your career options?

Not really, I said.

She handed me an application for nursing school at Camosun College and said I was different from the other girls; I was more sensitive. I was ready for Change.

But she'd got me all wrong. I was sensitive as a rock. I'd watched Cassie and Amber slice themselves and said nothing. I just sat there, cruel and useless. What kind of fool just sits there? I should have said I was impressed. I should have said I was sorry. I just should have. Said something kind.

*　　*　　*

The doctor at White Oaks was no help either.

I asked him for a sedative because I couldn't sleep. The opera never comes.

He said there was no reason for me to be tranquilized.

Look, I said, I've got a particular disease. You might not have heard of it before, but trust me, I've got it, and I'm probably gonna die.

What seems to be the problem?

The problem, I said, is this: I was born with a fever, and it's been gone since I was six, but it's started coming back to me this year. It comes and goes. I can't ever predict. I'll be burning and dizzy, and then it just leaves. When I woke up in the middle of last night, I was covered in cold sweat.

He put his hand on my forehead, then stuck a glass tube under my tongue.

Hold it, he said. Press down.

After a while, he took the thermometer from my pressed lips. We watched as the red line rose. It fell; it rose again slowly.

98.7 degrees, he said. You have no temperature, young lady. You're perfectly fine.

You're perfectly fine.

He said he was hip to that old chestnut, the fever ruse.

Fever's a symptom, he informed me. One is not born with a fever.

But I was—

Fever is not a disease, he said. The enemy most often takes the form of a virus or an infection. And fever, he said, fever is nature's way of removing her enemy.

A GOOD GIRL

WHEN I wouldn't tell anyone where my parents were, they sent me to see a placement officer.

Her name was Hazel; she liked to bet on greyhound dogs. Next year, when she turned sixty, she planned to move to Florida so she could bet all day long.

You can smoke if you want, she said. I'm cool.

We had our little chat.

I told Hazel I wanted to be a nurse.

That's a good goal, she said.

And it was. The thought of nursing school gave me such a feeling of purpose. Wearing all that white, I would feel pure. The scars and the tar, the bushes and Bacardi bottles, the taste of Dirk Wallace, the sight of silent blood from a razor blade, all of these would fade forever when I donned my white uniform. In my soft white-soled shoes, I would tend to wounded men just like Everly. My mother used to comfort men with bullet wounds and acid flashbacks. I knew I could do the same. When I bandaged wounds, I'd whisper, *Everything will be fine.*

* * *

They all get gold stars for ridding me of my antisocial tendencies. Take me off the streets where I met thieves and whores. Put me in a home where I can watch *Dynasty* and eat steak.

The Mickelsons, Hazel said, are a wonderful family. They live in Gordon Head.

Broken locks and bruised knees and borrowed lip gloss and rain on the streets.

Ivy Mercer lived in Gordon Head. She lived in a mansion high on a cliff. Maybe she lived next door to the Mickelsons.

Hazel had files stacked on her desk. I wasn't tempted to see whether she had one on Justine. It seemed so strange to me that you could have this image in your mind, as present as a cross of hope worn around the neck, and then you could just let it go.

Hazel opened a file.

She handed me a map.

This is the Red Zone, she said, and there it was. The streets of downtown, Yates and Douglas and Pandora and Government shaded in red while the rest of Victoria was redless and white.

These maps are usually given to girls on probation, Hazel said, but I would still like you to stay out of the Red Zone. And I'd like you to have no contact with any of these people.

She handed me a list. Geronimo Thomas, Luce Tathers, Michael John Burns . . . I didn't know any of those guys. They were probably pimps.

I just want to be a nurse, I said. I don't want to go downtown anymore. I want to live in Gordon Head.

Good. And do something positive for yourself, Sara.

Like what?

Get involved in the Y. Join the drama club.

Sure, I said.

But secretly I was thinking that Hazel wasn't too bright, because if she knew what I knew, her eyes would be full of tears and she would never presume recreational activities could be my remedy.

Hazel said the Mickelsons were expecting me for supper. At 6:00, she said. Gillian makes a mean steak. Don't be late. They're expecting you.

She wrote their address and phone number on my map: 3765 Houlihan Lane.

I will. *Be a good girl. I will. I will.*

You're an easy case, she said. I wish all my girls were so ready for change.

You believe me?

Of course I do.

You think I can become a nurse?

You can do anything you want, Sara. But you'll have to graduate from high school first.

Sure, I said. But I was thinking to myself that Camosun College better make an exception for me. Gloria was on my side. The only way I was going back to Mount Drug was with a gun in my hand.

You think I'll make a good nurse, Hazel?

Terrific, she said, and she circled a name from her list of potential champion dogs.

*   *   *

I know you think I'm going to fuck up the Mickelsons. Chapter Ten: Fire in Gordon Head. So go ahead and doubt me. I don't care. Just fuck off.

It was the first day of June, and the sky was still sunless and white.

It was 4:00. I thought I should just get on a bus near the Social Services office.

As I walked toward the bus stop, men no longer gave me lewd looks. Three days in White Oaks, I'd lost the necessary innocence. I still wore China's white coat and her white flimsy dress; I still wore her lace-up leather boots. As for the knife, you'll have to take a guess. OK, I still had my knife, but I swear I wasn't planning on using it.

In two hours, the Mickelsons would give me a new wardrobe. We'd have a hearty steak dinner—my first taste of blood and meat. Before dinner, we'd probably say a prayer. After dinner, I'd retreat to the guest room, where I wouldn't touch myself.

Broken locks and bruised knees and borrowed lip gloss and rain on the streets. I wouldn't write in my notebook. 'Cause if I wrote the words, the images would come rushing back to me. I'd get a sudden urge for rooftops and alleys. I'd want to climb out the window.

So I'd leave my notebook alone. I'd read the Bible. It was about time. Maybe I'd read *Little House on the Prairie.* I was pretty sure the Mickelsons would have the collected works of Laura Ingalls Wilder. I wanted to read those books. I swear. I'm not kidding you. Really, I'm not being insolent.

*   *   *

The thought of nursing school filled me with such good, clean energy, I could barely keep still. I wanted to yell at every stranger, *I have motivation, I have ambition, I have a plan!* Ronald

Reagan started that war with Grenada, and maybe I could go there and help the wounded Southern boys shot down by Commie bastards.

I walked by the bus stop.

Would it be rude to arrive before six? Yeah, it probably would. I should try to kill time productively. I could have pushed a tourist the way China did. I could have spat on all the nature kids in their stupid Birkenstocks. I could have got arrested like my mother, but I was a good girl now so sever me from the family tree.

*   *   *

At a Chinese market, lilies bloomed in white plastic pails. I chose a pale pink bouquet for my temporary mom and dad. I paid for the flowers with my Fresh Start allowance.

I had one hour left to kill and I knew where I wanted to go.

First thing, I went to McDonald's, where I ordered a milk shake and headed upstairs to the bathroom to check on my face. In White Oaks, I'd dreamed of cutting my hair like Cassie's, drawing black lines under my eyes, wearing fishnet stockings with fighter's boots. Cassie told me her skinhead friends hung around in the gutters below the Empress Hotel. I loved the names of the bands she listened to. The Exploited, The Damned. Maybe, at last, I would have heard music I liked, but I wasn't going to the gutters. I looked no worse for wear in the mirror, only slightly startled, the way someone looks when a fist is heading straight for her eyes.

HIPPIES SUCK was written on the bathroom wall. I was

tempted to write AND SO DO YOU. Lipstick vandalism, trait of a White Oaks alumni.

Two boppy, giggly girls were pouring Southern Comfort into their plastic cups of 7Up. They smelled like Chantilly.

They were giggling about how Pete and Mark were just so cute.

Oh my God, they are so cute. I gave the twinkies a dirty look, but they didn't shut up. I sent them a message via ESP. Stop giggling. Shut the fuck up. But they just kept giggling as they drank their spiked soda pop. They were really irritating me.

A good girl would like these girls.

A good girl would wish them luck with Pete and Mark.

A good girl wouldn't want to smash them into the wall.

And I was a good girl now.

At 5:15, a red double-decker bus passed me and a man with a megaphone announced that the stone building on the left was erected in 1835. I thought that when I was rehabilitated, I would apply for a job driving one of those buses. I could show those tourists some sights. Here's the King's Hotel, a former saloon during the gold rush and now a place where a girl named Alice gets paid if she acts like a whore. Above the building erected in 1835 is a roof where a girl with blond hair sleeps 'cause she's got no home. Welcome to Victoria, City of Gardens. Here's a gutter, here's a straitjacket; here's a bed of tar and stone.

But tourists see what they want to see. In Grade Nine, I had to do Work Experience at Native Expressions, one of those tourist stores. I sold little dolls supposedly made by local Indian girls, but really they were made in China. My boss made me cut the labels off.

It was funny walking by the same store now. The windows were full of Princess Di crap. The future Queen—her face was on tea towels and T-shirts and china plates. I didn't really see what Princess Di had to do with Victoria. I guess it was just because we were named after another Queen. I don't know why but it always got on my nerves that we were living in this hick town of loggers and headbangers, and somehow we were supposed to act like we were some lovely British village. Personally, I didn't give a fuck about Princess Di, and just seeing her prissy face all over the place put me in a bad mood. I wanted to smash into my old workplace and set every towel on fire. Once Queen Elizabeth came to Victoria and we got the day off school. Dean took acid and I hot-knived some hash with Heather, and the three of us went down to the Empress Hotel. Heather really wanted to see the Queen, and she pulled me to the front of the crowd. The Queen wasn't wearing a crown and she looked just like she does on postcards, regal and supreme. I saw her. She didn't see me. She waved from inside her armored car. Some girl yelled out, Death to the monarchy! and now that I think about it, the voice was familiar. Yeah, the girl who lipped off the Queen, I know that was Justine.

*   *   *

You'll never guess where I went.

The Greater Victoria Public Library.

Yeah, party time.

I'd decided to teach myself to be a nurse. I'd get my own degree. I didn't need anybody to certify me. I'd resuscitate the dead. I'd learn the secrets of breathing. With all my aptitude, I might even invent a new kind of CPR.

I'd show them all.

I asked the chick at the help desk where the books on fever were.

Books on fever, she said sarcastically, what exactly do you mean?

I mean the disease, you fool. Haven't you heard of the disease that's licking through my veins? I can't wait till I die because then they'll do an autopsy, and all those idiots will finally believe that there really was so much warmth inside of me.

I found what I was looking for in the card catalog. FN 112. *Fever of Unknown Origin*. Some doctor had actually written my auto-biography.

It was a pretty fascinating book, especially for me, a girl who didn't really like to read. The book described exactly what had happened to me in the bathrooms of the King's and Le Gardin.

Violent chills are impressive—the cold sensation almost identical with freezing, all the muscles convulsed in a frenzy of shivering contractions, the teeth chattering with tension, the whole body bent in a fetal position, the skin pale, the hair on end, the heart beating rapidly. Patient is overcome with extreme anguish.

In 1679, some doctor named Sydenham discovered fever, and he wrote a better version of what the quack doctor at White Oaks told me:

Fever is nature's engine which she brings into the field to remove her enemy.

I loved the line, though I didn't know why. I wrote it down in my notebook. I didn't think anything of it at the time. I just thought, This is my notebook, a place where I can write a phrase I love.

But now I regret writing because the cop took my notebook. And they probably think fever is a code because of what me and Justine did. They think I premeditated my crime only because I loved writing the words: *remove her enemy.*

At 5:45, I looked out the library window and saw Ivy Mercer's green Volvo. I was pretty sure it was her mother's car. It seemed like a sign. With library books in my hand, I thought I'd politely ask Mrs. Mercer if she minded driving me to the Mickelsons' in Gordon Head. On the drive to the serene suburb, I would tell her how much I admired her daughter. Because I did admire Ivy. She also made me sick with jealousy.

Ivy was not meant for Mount Drug; she looked so out of place, with her olive skin and flat chest and unfeathered hair. But I liked the way she looked, with her immense blue eyes and bowl-cut brown hair and corduroy floods. When she walked by the foyer, her forehead would furrow as if she was concentrating furiously on an idea. I don't know if she heard Mackie tell her she was a two, but she gave the impression that his ratings meant nothing to her.

I could probably find her father's books in the library. He was a famous lawyer who I'd seen on TV talking about the rights of the indigenous people. I'd heard he'd made a lot of money because they turned his book *The Salish Tribe* into a CBC miniseries. Ivy's mother was a former model who lived in Paris during the riots of '68. I knew all about the Mercers because every time the newspaper did one of those Prominent People in Our City stories, there would be a big photo of the Mercer family in their glass Gordon Head home. Ivy's father looked very wise as he posed beside carved statues. Behind him was an eight-foot-high window with a view of the ocean far below. Ivy's mother, she was a young wild bride, like Everly, but obviously she didn't drag her family into some free-love commune.

Once, in art class, Ivy made the mistake of boasting quietly about how she'd been Accepted to Smith College. She was going to study poetry just like Sylvia Plath, her heroine. If you admire poet chicks so much, Dale said, why don't you just cut to the chase and stick your head in the oven? The burnouts all thought that was pretty funny. I probably laughed too because at the time I was still trying to fit in. But really, I couldn't believe someone in our school planned to do something like study poetry in a famous school in America. It seemed so hard to believe. Even though I'd laughed at her, after school I followed Ivy out to the parking lot. I watched. Her mother drove up in a green Volvo. I caught a glimpse of Mrs. Mercer sympathetically tousling Ivy's hair as if to say, It's almost over, darling, soon you'll be out of this hellhole. During the next week, I followed Ivy to the parking lot every day. I lingered, not sure of what I wanted to say. I just looked at her as she waited for her ride. Climbing into the green Volvo with her canvas knapsack jaunty on her back, she'd kiss her mother on the cheek. Maybe she said to her mother, There's the girl who never says a word in class. I think she's a retarded mute.

Hey, Ivy, I said to her the next day, two words that took all my strength and nerve. She looked down at her shoes, black leather boystyle Oxfords, and didn't smile or wave. Like all the girls at Mount Drug, she really didn't want anything to do with me.

But now that I was good, maybe I could hang out with her. After dinner at the Mickelsons', she would help me with my college application form.

Hey, I yelled when I saw Mrs. Mercer in the newspaper room. She was reading the *New York Times.*

She looked up at me. She had no idea who I was. She stared at my fur coat and then she looked down at my high heels.

I know your daughter. I know Ivy. How's she doing?

She's well. Busy.

Where's that college she's going to?

It's in New England.

She's really lucky.

Lucky? She's worked tremendously hard.

I know. I mean, I know that she's so smart. That's why she's lucky to be getting off this island.

I didn't really know what to say. I could tell that Mrs. Mercer didn't like the looks of me. And I was suddenly shy around her. I couldn't believe I had ever considered asking her for a drive to Gordon Head. The way she was looking at me, and her smooth black hair, and those very high cheekbones, and her necklace of clean black pearls.

Well, I just wanted you to tell Ivy I said hello. You know, good luck.

Yes, I'll tell her, she said, but she looked annoyed. What's your name?

Justine.

OK, Justine. I'll pass along the message.

She didn't smile or anything and she gave me this look which was so knowing as if she looked at me and saw Cassie's cut on

my arm and the knife in my boot and the fact that I'd never finished my paper on *Lord Jim*.

I found about five hundred books on nursing, and I checked out
a couple with diagrams. *Nursing: A Noble Profession* by Dr. Emma
Forester. I chose that one because the cover had a drawing of
this kinky-looking lady with a 1950s beehive.

By the time I'd paid Seamus's overdue fines it was 6:15. So I
went to call the Mickelsons just to let them know I was on my
way. *Hey, I've been in the library talking to the Prominent Mrs. Mercer and
I'm sorry I'm late but I'm on my way.* Really, that's what I was planning to say.

Only in the room with pay phones I noticed that there were
telephone books from every state in America. So say, for example, you wanted to look up your mother in Palm Springs, you
could. You'd just walk over to the Palm Springs phone book and
pull the heavy book off the shelf and bite your nails as you sat
down on a heating vent.

So you look up Caglio because that was the Leader's last
name. You've been telling everybody that you didn't know your
mother's whereabouts, but you've known his name all along.
You just didn't want a stranger calling your mother and telling
her you were passing out in bathrooms.

So you walk to the pay phone and dial the number collect.

You hope that he will answer. Because you've always wanted
to talk to Him. Thanks, asshole, for running a cult. Thanks for
the orgies. Thanks for running off to Palm Springs with the
money you stole from the Workers' Co-op Fund.

But say, for example, a woman answers and you try to find

your kind voice and not sound like the sullen little bitch everyone has told you you've become.

Sara, she said, Saarrrraaaa.

And her voice was still honeylike; the voice of a woman
who'd always been loved.

Yeah, it's me. Your daughter.

There was silence.

Oh my God, I—hold on, honey.

Then I heard a watery sound. It could have been the sound of a
waterfall. Or liquor being poured into a glass. Or a body diving
into the warm turquoise water of a swimming pool. It was a
smooth, watery sound, not like the water I usually heard. On my
island, the sounds of water are rough waves smashing against
rocks. But my mother's water was smooth, and while I waited
for her to come back to the phone, I listened carefully for five
minutes, trying to convince myself she was just mixing a drink
or taking a swim, but finally the operator came on and said I'd
been disconnected and would I like to make another call.

So much for my mother.

She probably heard it in my voice. I hadn't accomplished anything.

Honey, hold on.

I bit the inside of my lip real hard and imagined a waterfall in
my stupid, screwed-up, useless mind. The waterfall was pure
and rushing down, and it was washing out the sound of her
water, washing away her honeylike voice, calling me honey like
she used to do when she really was my mother and she'd get lazy
and high and touch my long hair which she loved to braid when
I was a child and she was really my mother and I was kind.

STAR SKATER STAR

IT was better this time, better than in the garden, because he was real, real and rough, as he pressed his body down onto mine. His mouth took away the metallic taste of Dirk Wallace; his hands made me forget all about my mother's silent good-bye.

It was better than with Dean, because he wasn't lazy and slow; he was jagged and brisk, this man with scrapes all over his elbows and knees, this man who really seemed to want me to stay in his apartment, who held me, begged me not to meet my Gold Star family.

I've seen you around downtown, he said. You always look so—

So tough, I hoped he'd say. So intimidating, so dangerous, so mean.

So lost, he said, kissing my neck. You always looked like you were looking for something. He stopped touching me and asked me this: What were you looking for?

Just a feeling, I said, moving his hand back down to where it had been.

*   *   *

I was happy with him, so much happier than I would have been with the helpful Mickelsons. In his dirty bathroom, he helped me disguise. I hacked my hair with his dull scissors. Strands floated down like feathers to the floor.

He bleached all my redness away. Stinging sensation on my scalp; soon my hair was whiter than bone, white as porcelain.

Speed: he kept a stash in a Wonder Bread bag. He sliced open the shiny pills he called black beauties. When the white powder was on my stomach, he snorted it up, let me lick his finger to taste the remains. This might be a cure, I thought, feeling a sudden startle that wasn't fever but a kick-start. This might be a cure, I thought, one better than any dumbass doctor could prescribe. This might be a cure, hearing him say, *You're my kind of girl. I love runaways.*

I kissed him for hours that night, thinking maybe it was meant to be. I'd met him so easily.

I guess you could say I picked Nicholas up. I went for it as soon as I saw him skating down and soaring off the skinny rail by the steps leading away from the library. A cop told him to get off public property, and Nicholas said, Fuck off.

He said it, he didn't mumble under his breath.

Hey, I yelled out, and he came my way. His hair was spiky and black; his smile brattier than Dean's. He hitched up the torn jeans falling off his hipbones. He smiled like he believed me when I told him I was training to be a nurse and could cure all his injuries.

*   *   *

On my second day, I noticed the Blue House.

I was sitting on his windowsill, reading in my borrowed books about tourniquets and iodine.

Nicholas lived in a neighborhood called Fairfield, which is about five miles from downtown. In the clear. It was a hidden-away neighborhood I'd never been to before, and I was surprised by it because it was even more run-down than the street where I lived with my dad. Here the houses were all slammed together on sideways streets. The tiny backyards were without apple trees or rosebushes, just discarded junk—a sagging couch, a deflated kiddie pool, mangled motorbikes, all brown and rotting and rainsoaked. It was obviously a neighborhood for derelicts, a place I should have felt I belonged.

And the house that caught my eye seemed to have a kind of dirty grandeur. It was the highest on the hill, shoved behind a smaller house. There was something almost human about it, hovering behind like the older brother, the bully, the lurking boy.

The rotting wood of the house was painted blue, not sky blue, but dark blue, the blue of wet jeans and American police uniforms. The broken windows were covered with Saran Wrap; an A in a red circle was spraypainted on the front door. I stared at the house, and after a few minutes, I saw a girl. A girl who must have come from the Empress gutters, 'cause she was dressed just like Cassie, with a shaved head, a fringe of bangs, a body enveloped by a green army jacket. She gave the door a sudden kick. When no one answered, she shimmied up a rain pipe, and climbed in, head first, through the plastic pane of the window. I saw the soles of her black boots rise up against the window's edge. Then she vanished, and the sky seemed whiter and duller than it had ever been before.

I went back to reading about arteries. Must be the speed, I thought, because I just could not concentrate.

That night, I asked Nicholas about the Blue House.

Don't go there, he ordered.

Why not? I said. It looks like something fun is going on inside.

It's skanky, he said. It's disgusting.

Nicholas had been around or so he liked to say. He'd been to California twice; he even lived in San Francisco for six weeks when he was my age. A sneaker company paid for his trips; he skated in contests; he said he was *legendary*. Now he was twenty-three; he was still a skateboard star; he sold speed on the side and had gouged cheekbones and almost gold eyes and all the little boys who adored him called him Skills. *Just trust me. You don't want to go inside.*

* * *

The Uplands mansion was white with smooth pillars rising on either side of the clean entrance door. All the lights were off; the owner was a Hollywood producer who was always in L.A. The moon lit up the concrete curves of his swimming pool. I lay back on the wealthy man's lawn chair, wishing I wasn't so restless. All night, boys came through the carefully trimmed bushes, until there were fifteen of them, taking turns. They would stand in the shallow end of the drained pool, and then skate toward the deep end, riding up the smooth curves.

The boys' bodies threw huge shadows across the walls of the pool. Monsterlike, the shadows loomed with immense bent knees and raised arms. Though they'd never admit it, I bet those guys liked having their bodies become dark giants there in the quiet concrete valley of a rich man's waterless swimming pool.

As for me, I had nowhere for my restless energy. In my notebook, I tried to write a letter to my dad but my mind was racing too fast for words. I thought of Amber, sneaky and pretty. *Sara, you ain't ready to escape. Sara, you're almost ready to learn.* What did that mean? I really wished she was around, so we could break into the mansion, steal ourselves the jewels we deserved. I bet there were diamonds and emeralds inside; I would have liked to touch their shine. But it was for the best that I stayed still among fifteen rowdy boys. Two days had gone by, and I hadn't drunk anything. I had not hurt anyone.

*   *   *

Nicholas lived above a bicycle-repair shop that seemed shady. No one was ever there. He wouldn't explain, but I think his dealer was involved. Some of these details should be changed to protect the innocent, but I know you're not going to narc on Saint Nicholas.

Anyway, when we got to his front door, he fiddled with the lock while I glanced back at the Blue House. All the lights were on. Lush, violent music played. Three women lay together on the small patch of lawn. One had green hair; one wore a black lace dress; the third wore a black leather jacket and swung around a cane. They all looked like they were around twenty-one. Nicholas pushed me in through his doorway, but before I left the street, I caught a glimpse of their faces. Flushed faces, lipstick smeared, smiles secret and content.

*   *   *

In his bed, he warned me about my body like he'd warned me about the Blue House.

His touch was gentle and aimless; I thought it was the speed. He lost interest and blamed it on his destroyed tailbone. But I was ready, I was tired of the way we skimmed over each other's bodies.

You're not ready, he said.

Why not?

You're too young. You should save yourself until you're in love.

I'll never be in love.

It was true. I'd seen the Pleasure Family; I knew too much about love and I would never be that way.

You're a teenage girl. Falling in love is your whole deal.

But I don't want to be in love. I want—

Do you want to be ruined? Do you want to turn into a slut?

No, I said, but I'm—

Then stop asking for it. You're gonna get me in trouble. You're a baby, for Christ's sake. You're *jailbait*.

Can't we just—

But he turned his back to me. He didn't like to argue. He laid down the law. That was his way.

While he slept, I touched the scars on his back. Nicholas's scars came from concrete and pavement; they were proof of his prowess. They weren't really scars to me. Scars were words cut with paper clips and X-Acto knives and razor blades. How could he think I was some innocent when I was the one who'd seen flowers burned into breasts, words cut into thighs? Mr. Champion, he'd fallen off a fifty-foot ramp and split in two, been sewn up, and now he was seamed like a teddy bear. I'd asked him if his fall hurt, thinking of Cassie and Amber. *It feels really good. It feels like sex.* Yeah, it hurt, he said, it fucking killed, but that's OK 'cause they put me on the morphine drip.

Restless with lust, I crawled out of his bed and tiptoed over to the window.

I pulled the curtain back.

The lights of the Blue House were still on, and the woman in the black lace dress was there, lolling about on the lawn by herself, as if she was being felt up by some invisible embrace. She looked pretty ridiculous. He's right, I thought, they're all skanks over there. Just go to sleep.

And I did sleep. Until around five in the morning, when I was woken up by the desperate, drunken voice of a girl. Her voice was singsong, rough and sweet, so familiar I thought it was a dream.

Luce! the girl sang urgently, like she'd kill herself if he didn't obey. Let me in, Luce!

I wrapped my arms around my boyfriend, hoping he might wake up and hold me back. In my dreams, I went to a funeral and Justine was no longer singing because she was dead.

*   *   *

In the morning, I was more determined than ever to be a nurse. My face in the mirror was pale white, Kabuki white, no longer flushed and fiery. And get this: he'd stolen me a nurse's outfit from Goodwell Uniforms. White stockings and white-

soled shoes. I'd screamed when he gave it to me, and he'd
held me by my hips and twirled me around. I looked pretty,
but I didn't care. Secretly, I hoped the nurse outfit might turn
him on.

I read of tourniquets and iodine.

*A tourniquet is a wide band of cloth placed around an extremity. It is then
tightened until the blood flow is cut off. The amount of pressure necessary typi-
cally causes vascular and nerve trauma. Thus a tourniquet should only be used to
save a life at the expense of possibly sacrificing a limb.*

I knew I'd make such a great nurse. Who else could handle all
this gruesome stuff?

While I studied, Nicholas watched skate contest videos.

That's Christian Hosoi, he said, do you know who he is?

Yeah, I know.

(Fast forward) That's Steve Caballero. Sara, check out his
frontside inverts.

(Fast forward) That's me, Nicholas Haven. Watch this, Sara!
This is where the crowd goes wild for my whole run. (Fast forward)

I caught glimpses: boys with their shirts off, their chests like
his, bony and smooth.

I tried to distract him. Offered to take off my uniform if he'd
turn off the TV.

No way, you look good in that dress. You look pure.

I'm not pure, I said. I lost my innocence in the King's Hotel.

Don't make me laugh, he said.

I sat on his lap, lifted his shirt, bit a hickey, a red mark to add
to his temporary scars.

You don't look like a nymphomaniac, he said.

Oh, and what do I look like?

He pushed the white bangs from my forehead, traced the lines of my face.

An Ice Queen.

*   *   *

Neighborhood boys came by to cop speed. Scotty, this one kid, he probably wasn't even thirteen. He'd cut slits in his eyebrows. That was Nicholas's trademark, back in his champion days. Scotty's jeans sagged just like Nicholas's, but Nicholas wasn't trying; he was just skinny because speed takes away your appetite. Scotty stared wide-eyed at Nicholas, as if he wasn't sure he deserved to be in the same room.

Hey, Scotty, I asked, when Nicholas was in the bathroom, do you know some guy named Luce?

The guy across the street? Yeah, I know him.

What's he like?

He's a fag, Scotty said. As if that was the end of the conversation. As if that was all he needed to say.

Well, what's going on over there? Why are all those women— Nicholas came out of the bathroom.

Who's a fag? he asked, yanking Scotty's skateboard viciously.

Luce.

Luce, Nicholas scoffed, that guy's a poseur. He's a puff.

Around his admirers, Nicholas was more affectionate. He'd put his hand up my top; he'd hold me in his arms. But now he shunned me because I'd committed the sin of asking Scotty about the one place he did not want me to go.

What was the big deal? It made no sense to me. Nicholas could talk for hours about his former days as a dropout vandalist renegade. Pissing on cop cars, throwing headbangers through the plate-glass windows of department stores. He could listen to songs where the only words were kill *destroy* kill and fuck *society*. But when it came to me, or the Blue House, he had this sudden obsession with purity.

You guys, just tell me what's going on over there. I won't—

Hey, Scotty, you want me to re-grip your board?

Yeee-ah! Scotty gushed.

That way you can move faster, Nicholas said.

Yeah, Scotty said dreamily, that way I can really speed.

After Scotty left, I took more speed to stave off the hollow, crashing wave of chemical sadness, and then I got cranky and restless. I ran laps around his bed.

Why don't you go for a walk? he suggested. You seem pretty hyper.

I might get caught.

You won't get caught, he insisted.

I've got a guy named Dirk Wallace who wants to bust up my face!

Sara, you're paranoid. Get out of here for a while.

He ran his hands over the wheels of his skateboard. Here we go, I thought, I had a real knack for driving people away.

Where am I supposed to go?

Don't go downtown. Just go home and see if that Sylvia chick is still around.

Should I come back?

Of course, he said, tousling my hair. I can't sleep without my runaway.

*   *   *

Truthfully, I was glad to be out of his apartment. Outside, there was a rough wind and the sky was dusky and violet. I wandered around the lanes behind the broken homes, kicking the gravel and hoping for a storm. I knew where I wanted to go, and it was useless to fight the lure.

By the time I reached the door of the Blue House, I was breathless. I'd never been so excited in my entire life. My heart was beating so quick and loud, I felt it might slam straight through my skin. I had entered so many places in the last week, slept in four strange beds, and with every intrusion—into Ming's, into the alley, into the diner, into the King's, into Ledger, into White Oaks, into a skater's bed—I'd grown bolder and braver. A year might have gone by. A year since I sat in the bushes, mute and useless. Nervous and silent when I was at Ming's, now I was rowdy and hectic and sure. Sure this would be the best place I'd ever found. Sure, I was sure.

I knocked on the door.

Who's there? a woman said. She sounded leery and suspicious, and behind her I heard a brash, mocking laugh. Did they have a peephole? Could they see me, standing there in my nurse's uniform? What was I doing?

All his warnings came back to me. Him and Scotty had told me about the Blue House, their stupid, far-fetched tall tales. Sacrificial virgins, white slavery, black leather whips and chains.

It must have been the comedown from speed because all my excitement suddenly turned to white-hot fear. I would go inside and be destroyed. The wolf dressed up like a grandmother. My, what pretty eyes you have.

I ran away from the Blue House, ran as fast as I could. The sky was thick with rain now, and I had to push through the black, wet sky. I heard a voice in my head. *You stupid, fucked-up girl. You almost fucked up the best thing you had.* My white dress was soaked. Under the streetlight, I could see my breasts and the bones of my hips. Shivering, I couldn't wait to be back in his bed. He was a good guy, careful and kind, so unlike Bryce and Dean. I'd climb the stairs quietly. I'd apologize. I should have trusted him, listened to his warning. I don't know what possessed me, I just always want to go where I'm not supposed to go. He'd warm me up. We'd go to bed; I wouldn't beg; I'd stop pushing him; I'd win his love.

I took off my shoes, walked up the stairs silently. I wanted my repentant return to be a surprise. His door was unlocked, and I tiptoed across his kitchen floor so softly, I might have been a ghost.

Someone moaned in his bedroom.

Nicholas was sitting on the windowsill, his hands in fists, his head thrown back, his mouth open as he moaned again. And before him, on his knees, was a bare-chested boy in blue jeans. Who was it, I didn't even care. Could have been Scotty. Could have been any of the boys who'd skated in the swimming pool. Later, I'd think about all the boys I'd seen that night, and I'd remember Devon, a freckled kid with a bleached crew cut and a cute, chip-toothed grin. It was Devon in the bedroom, Devon who'd once handed Nicholas his brand-new skateboard, his voice breaking as he'd asked for an autograph.

Nicholas would be so embarrassed if he knew what I'd seen. He'd feel the same shame I'd felt when my father discovered me. I couldn't handle it at all.

When I put China's coat on, I started to cry, and I grabbed all the speed from the Wonder Bread bag. Who cares, I thought, I'm back to my bad ways. Where was my knife? My mind was racing and I was fighting the sudden urge to scream. I'd have to leave my library books behind. Sue me. Mr. Pro could artfully throw them in the slot as he went flying through the air in a wondrous ollie kickflip leap of faith.

This time, I looked maniacal as I knocked on the Blue House door. My crazed expression would turn out to be handy; I'd fit right in. Knock, knock, knock. Who's there? It's Little Red Riding Hood.

I just wanted to party.

Luce! I screamed, in perfect imitation. Let me in! Luce!

The door opened. Blame it on that. The door opened, and so I went inside. You probably think I shouldn't have, but where else was I going to go? Where I'm not supposed to go is where I'm supposed to go, if that makes any sense at all. By now, I think you know what I mean.

THE BLUE HOUSE

I CRASHED the party in my nurse's uniform, swallowing
stolen speed as I moved down the long, dark, crowded hallway.
Inside, I acted very nonchalant—hey guys, waving at a few
strangers—so I wouldn't give away that I was there without the
vaguest kind of invite. I made a beeline for the kitchen, where I
knew I could find a bottle, because amphetamines weren't
enough; I wanted to get smashed. Minding the kitchen door
was Nicholas's nemesis, the notorious Luce, who was supposedly the anti-Christ but seemed pretty harmless to me. Aren't
you Nicholas's newest girlfriend? he said sarcastically, and then
he broke out into this caterwaul of a laugh. Go ahead and laugh
at me, I thought. The joke's on you, buddy. You're gonna wake
up in the morning with a dead body in your house.

Let me offer you a drink, he said. You look a little *déshabillé*.
Have you ever had Aquavit? he said, pouring me a colorless

liquor, which I drank in one swig because all the speed left me parched. You're Scandinavian, aren't you?

Norwegian, I said. From the hinterlands.

Oh yes, the hinterlands.

He wasn't put off by my sullen way, which was a pleasant change. My last night on the planet, it would be a relief to not have to fake being sweet. Pasty-faced and paunchy, Luce swept around like an overweight superhero. He was the kind of guy I would have liked to pal around with because he was so jolly.

Norwegian Queen, he said, be sure to come upstairs to the second floor for a little treat.

He gave me the creeps a little then, the way he said that, but I just poured myself some more of the colorless drink. *Upstairs for a little treat.* Sure, I said, but to myself I was thinking, Fuck off, poseur. As I'm sure you can understand, I didn't trust anybody anymore. Besides, I had bigger plans up my sleeve.

I walked around the living room and the bedrooms and the back porch, just picking up other people's glasses and downing their backwash.

It was a pretty debauched scene inside that house.

I saw some stuff I was probably too young to see.

All those debauched people were pretty proud of themselves. You could just tell. They moved around as if they were in some secret golden castle.

I was doing my best to look like I belonged, which isn't easy when you're falling facedown on the floor. Which is what I did. I tripped on the air. When I sat up, the whole room was spinning and I forced myself to focus on Gramps. Gramps was seriously trashed himself and seemingly senile, and the skinhead girl I'd seen scurrying up the rain pipe was making out with him. That made no sense to me at all. His hair was white, as white as mine, and his bones were frail. Maybe he was handsome once, maybe he was a war hero—Victoria's full of those veteran guys. Still, I couldn't stop staring. The skinhead girl was only wearing fishnets so you could see her pink underwear. So much for asking her if she knew the whereabouts of Justine. With her hips, she pushed herself into Gramps. Clearly, she was preoccupied. I had a lot of problems, but at least I wasn't necking with ninety-year-old men.

Two British guys cornered me when I tried to walk over to a sofa.

At least, I thought they were British because I was too drunk to catch on they were playing me for a fool. Wow, you're from London, really? I said. What's it like? I've always wanted to go there.

Bloody brilliant. Come upstairs with us lads. Come on up to the second floor.

What was the big deal with the second floor?

You look a little intimidated. Don't be intimidated by the fact that you're the youngest girl here.

Then they started talking about me like I'd stepped out of some skin magazine. *I could ride you so hard; I could break you in two; I could lick your pink little clit; I could do what your daddy doesn't want you to do.* I guess they thought I'd be seduced by the British accents, but I wasn't turned on.

I used to hate that girls had to be careful when they got drunk. That wasn't fair. Guys could get as wasted as they wanted, but girls always had this warning voice. Fuck that—I willed the warning voice away. I just kept on drinking other people's drinks. I'd worked out a good routine. Stand near a cup, and after a few minutes grab it and chug it down. I figured that if I got caught, I'd just open my eyes really wide and say I was so sorry in a little-girl voice.

I wanted to talk to the woman in the black lace dress who I'd seen lolling about on the front lawn and find out what she'd taken to make herself feel so good. That's another thing. I was always so afraid of feeling lovey-dovey and sexed-up, because I used to go to beach parties where girls would drink too much and they'd make complete fools of themselves, but I figured I wasn't about to turn soft and girly now, after all I'd been through. It used to be my worst fear that I'd say I love you in a slurred way.

Luce was like a pasha on the couch, women at his side and at his feet. I went to ask him for more Aquavit, but I fell into his lap and he wrapped his chubby arms around my waist.

My house is a church and we all pray to some God, Luce said, and then he stuck a needle into his arm. I watched, waiting for him to smile or let out a sigh, but there was nothing on his face. His eyes just closed and his head rolled to the side. The girl beside him, she should be in a museum painting, with her aquiline nose and sleek bobbed black hair. She looked so elegant and composed; she was probably twenty-five. I couldn't imagine any man ever saying anything lewd to her. I moved a little closer. Here's what I wanted to do: work up the nerve. To ask her to adopt me. What could she say? If I begged. You look so elegant and refined. I know I look like a hosebag, but I can change. I drafted a letter to her in my mind. Could you help me out? Could you give me some advice? I know I look serene, but it's the product of bleach, and hard work, just teaching myself not to feel which is good because why care about people when they're just going to turn out to be cruel? Well, I'm sure you have lots of advice, just a few phrases that don't include the words: recreational activities. Maybe you could recommend a good book—you look well read. I've read *Flowers in the Attic* and *The Other Side of Midnight* and *Go Ask Alice* and I don't want to read any more books where the girl dies in the end. Perhaps you could recommend one, but not the ones we read in school, not *Lord Jim* or *Lord of the Flies* or *Lord of the Rings*, because I can't get into any of those Lord guys. Maybe you could take me to a movie I might enjoy. The last movie I saw was *Porky's* and everyone laughed their faces off and I just got so depressed. My boyfriend at the time, Dean Black, later gave me a lecture in his best friend's red pickup truck. Sara, that movie rules. Why are you so uptight? Sorry, I just hated that movie and I don't ever want to see a movie again. What else? Maybe you could tell me what kind of career you have because you look so glamorous and in control. Maybe you're a fashion designer visiting from New York. I could be your assistant—I'd work hard, I swear. *Just get me out of here.* No offense, but everyone on this island is a hick except for you and me. If you don't want to hire me, perhaps you could suggest a career because I really want to accomplish something that's not ordinary. I'm told I have an aptitude for the helping professions. I love certain words, like *licorice* and *lacerate*. That's not enough, I know. I know as well that if I was truly good my mother would love me and I would not carry around a knife in my notebook. I lie a lot lately. It used to be impossible, but now it comes so easily. I'm fucking smashed out of my mind. I'm trying to be a good person but everyone I meet has an iron heart. I've done some dastardly deeds. The worst thing my ex-boyfriend did was gang-rape a girl, who then tried to erase herself, and he and his friends laughed like they were watching a video game. They don't care, and though I've tried to make new friends, they're the only ones I have now. Tomorrow, they'll be waiting for me at my house and I could say no, I don't want to go to the forests with you, but truly, I'm scared 'cause when I stay in Victoria, I keep getting in trouble—like now I'm here and this Luce guy is sticking a needle in his arm and I promised him I'd go upstairs, where there's probably a white slavery auction or some sacrificial virgin rite. S & M, D & D. Don't think I don't know because I know what goes on here. I've been warned about Luce and his lascivious ways. I have a skimpy knowledge of tourniquets. *Just give me some advice.* The worst thing I ever did in the eyes of the world was steal money from a man who looked like Mr. Klein, my science teacher. No, the worst thing I did was not help Heather Hale. I took acid when I was six and I tripped while playing pin the tail on the donkey. I only read the dirty parts of *Forever*. I gave Bobby Schick blue balls. I walked in on an orgy when I was living in this commune, and I covered my eyes and stared. I stabbed a guy at my high school pep rally. I ditched the Mickelsons, a wonderful family who have done so much for wayward girls. I touched myself in my father's garden by the rosebushes he was cutting for me. And to be short and sweet, I didn't care and I don't care, not very much, and the only time I feel anything it's a sift of heat, which comes and goes and threatens to suffocate me. *Just help me, please.*

OK, she said kindly, wiping the tears from my eyes. Here's my advice. I don't want you to go to the logging camp because you deserve better than that. As for your latest plan for this evening, I think you should abandon it because at the moment you're in a vulnerable state of shock and in no shape to make such a fatal decision.

Actually, we never had this conversation because as soon as I turned to her, she lifted her palm toward the sky and held out her long white arm like an offering. Then she put the needle in herself and I looked away but saw her white fist punch hard her red vein. *Dear Abby: I finally met someone who looked like a role model and she turned out to be a fucking junkie! What should I do?*

*   *   *

I passed some passed-out girls with their skirts up past their knees, and if they could pass out here, I could too. Maybe. Maybe not. Do or die. Now or never.

It's funny. As soon as you even consider offing yourself, options appear. They're everywhere. Passing out seemed dull compared to slitting my wrists with a silver blade or swallowing the pile of gleaming black capsules. I wondered how Heather did it. I wanted to do it not in a girly way. Like maybe do something truly original and macabre. Hang myself from an oak tree so I'd dangle off the bedsheet tied around my neck; my body was so skinny now I'd be a white sliver waving from the boughs. Pistol to the head; shotgun to the brain. I bet no girl in Victoria's ever done that. I knew I wasn't going the head-in-the-oven route because they'd blame it on Sylvia Plath. Though I'd never read anything by Sylvia Plath, Ivy Mercer had given a paper on her life story in English class. Now that I was alone in the Blue House understanding the urge to off yourself, I realized I should have befriended Ivy when I had the chance. I just used to think girls like that would be disgusted by the marijuana plants in my house and the rumors of my sordid family history. It never occurred to me that I could lie, tell her I was from the Norwegian hinterlands or some such bullshit.

It was funny to think that Ivy was probably right now packing to go to New England, which is somewhere near New York, I think. Good for her. I hope she gets the hell out of here and becomes a famous poet, though she'll have to invent some stuff about the beauty of her youth since no one writes poetry about parking lots and burnout boys. She'll probably write about the beauty of this island where, alas, mist drifts over mountains. Who gives a fuck. I know that's what she'll do too because all the poems we read are about nature, which is so obviously beautiful I don't understand why you have to go to

an American college to learn about it and so I don't really wish
her luck after all, because I'm jealous, but also because Ivy had
been so busy trying to brownnose her way into college that she
failed to even notice the most tragic fact of our entire high
school year, which was this: Heather, the tough stoner girl
who drank her father's gin and kept tinfoil balls of hash in her
Maybelline, one day limped like an old man on his way to
death, and soon after she disappeared without a trace. *Erase.*

It killed me that Mr. Cool Star Skater Star had to have a morphine drip! I was sitting on the floor by these bald men in black
dresses when suddenly I thought of that and I just started to
laugh. That's when I overheard a conversation. I didn't mean to
eavesdrop. I was doing fine, drunkenly laughing to myself,
when I overheard:

The police are looking for her.

What'd she do this time?

She went too far, that's what she did.

At the time, the conversation was meaningless to me. Well,
actually, at first, I thought they might have been talking about
me. Could Dirk Wallace be ready to press charges against me
for humiliation and thievery? Could I be thrown in jail for fail-
ing to show up for a hearty steak dinner at the Mickelsons'? But
when I looked around the room, I realized there were hard-
ened criminals everywhere. I'm not joking. They could act
artsy all they wanted and paint their house blue and write *black
petal heart* on the bathroom wall, but the fact was they were all a
bunch of lousy degenerates. One woman with a pink mohawk
and a dog collar around her neck was right in front of me bragging about committing the felony of being a public nuisance.

She was just acting belligerent and boasting about how she spent her afternoon swinging around a baseball bat at the bingo hall. I didn't like her much. Then there was a prettier, frail girl on the couch who was covered in a sleeping bag, just like the one I'd seen on the roof. Her skin was in a bad condition, with a strange bursting red boil on her cheek, and she rubbed her eyes and asked me if I had some Percodan. I said I could give her some black beauties though she looked like she was in rough shape. The police could have been looking for her. I also talked to a guy who showed me his gun. He was in one of the bedrooms. I'd given up my desire for overdose and I was feeling kind of social and like I wanted to stir up some trouble again. Anyway, he showed me his gun, just a little pistol he'd picked up at the pawnshop. He said I could touch it. Can I *have* it? I replied.

Of course you can't have it.

Please, I said smiling. I begged him. Please give me your gun.

He was pretty handsome too, with greasy black hair and high cheekbones and a mean, dirty grin. Yeah, he was a mean man who'd done a stint in the maximum-security Mission jail. I kissed him on the mattress, and then later, when I bumped into him in the hall, I gave him a fake name, Josephine, which suited me more than Sara. I liked it so much that I didn't care when he called me a tease. So what—I'd been called worse. I'd been called a bitch and a slut, and even then, I knew none of those words were true. They were just words and they didn't mean anything. I'd forget them before I ever carved them into my skin. Look, Josephine, he said, I'll let you touch my gun.

I *want* it, I said. You don't understand.

We laughed a little. You're sure feisty, he said. You'd think you ran this town.

Can you get me some booze? I asked, and he did, and then I

asked him to come with me up to where my supposed treat was on the second floor.

What was the big deal? People were dancing in a bedless bedroom. I fell over and the guy with the gun caught me before I fell on my face. I loved the Blue House right then. So many strange-looking people dancing, all singing along to a song I'd never heard before. It was way better than the whole sock hop, slow-dance-to-Stairway-to-Heaven routine. Those deranged artsy types sure can dance. You should have seen them. I guess they were trying to dance like they were from New York or something. I wished China was with me because it would have killed her to see those girls in lace leggings twirling about with their serious, gloomy expressions.

The gun guy kept trying to get me to go dance with Gramps. Gramps was really getting down on the dance floor. I careened over to the old man because I wanted to give the gun guy a good laugh. I swayed my hips a little and smiled at the old man in this over-the-top-come-hither kind of way. I saw this girl dancing, and I moved closer to her because I liked the way she looked, haughty and sexy but not in a slutty way, and when I got closer to her, I realized she was me and I was looking at my reflection in the mirror. I looked like the kind of girl I'd always wanted to befriend.

So maybe I got a couple of lewd looks, but I kept thinking of those Mount Drug fools at their graduation dance, and at last, at least, I'd found something better.

The window was open and the breeze came in, and the smell of my city was bittersweet, salty, and at the same time clean.

It's funny how dancing with a bunch of strangers can make you realize how lonely and melancholy you've been, and now I felt so giddy and accepted, I even introduced myself to the girls in lace leggings. Snottily, they told me they were theater students, and I lied my face off, saying, Yeah, well, I'm going to Smith College in New England. Yeah, yeah, you're right, that's where Sylvia Plath went. I didn't want them thinking they were better than I was. Nice moves, I said. What do you call that kind of dance? Improv, they said snobbily. Got it. Improv, I snickered to the guy with the gun, who had started to follow me around and kept telling me it was time for me to go get my treat.

Sure, I said, but I tried to shake him, heading into another bedroom, where I flopped down on the mattress next to a couple of lovers who were naked under the sheets. A man with a face like Jesus and a Japanese girl with pigtails tied with shoelaces. He asked me to kiss her, and she blushed and rolled off of him.

Not that the naked Jesus guy cared, but I told him about my studies. Venous blood is impure, I said, and arterial blood is pure. Did you know that? I bet you didn't.

Tell me more, he said, and then he started shooting up, right there, next to me.

Here it comes, I knew. He would ask me if I wanted the needle and what would I say? I couldn't say I was sixteen and I was afraid of sharp objects breaking into my unscarred skin.

Little girl, his girlfriend said, haven't you ever done this before?

Sorry, I can't, I said. I've got this infectious disease. Perhaps you've heard of it. It's called typhoid.

That shut them up pretty quick. There was no way they would tell anybody I was naive.

I couldn't watch the needle go in because it reminded me of Amber slicing the soft skin near her thighs.

I thought I'd go find the skinhead girl in the pink underwear and see if I could crash with her in the Empress gutters because the gun guy was following me around and giving me this look from across the room. He seemed like the kind of guy who would get off on using disgusting words to a girl who's trying to act tough. That was one thing I've learned. Some guys get a power trip from making you uncomfortable and showing you up to be prim.

I wondered why I didn't have the guts to shoot up when I'd been bragging to myself about how I was brave enough to commit a macabre overdose. I'm a hypocrite.

The skinhead girl was gone, the frail girl on the couch told me. Wow, she said, you look like you've just had sex.

I told her I'd been dancing, but she didn't believe me. By the way, she said, her name's Denise. If you want to survive, don't call her skinhead girl.

What is this house? I wanted to ask. *How do you all know each other?*

Hey, she said suddenly, I seen you before. I seen you going into the Get Laid and Fight. You used to have long red hair, right? Man, I didn't recognize you. You've really changed.

Yeah, I was just a high school stoner kid back then.

Yeah, you've *really changed*. She sat up and kissed me on the cheek. For a second, I thought we were going to have a good talk about the sleaziness of Braun and the way I'd chosen China and she'd chosen me and now she was off learning to draw maps on the Dirk Wallace Scholarship Fund. We'd talk about the secret world of roofs and alleys and the greatest mystery of all, which was this: the whereabouts of Justine.

But she just whispered into my ear. Can you spare some change? Thanks man. I'm fucking dying I'm so hungry.

Because I had nowhere to sleep, I decided to head to the third floor, where I would open every door until I found an empty bedroom. I was getting tired of watching people shoot up, and most of the people left inside were drifting off into their dreamy inner opium den. No one was amused by my conversations about ventricular atrophy. Besides, the guy with the gun was shadowing me. I told him to meet me out on the porch, and then I ran up the stairs with a sudden burst of energy.

I opened the third and last door, just as I had opened the two others before.

At first, I thought she was a child, a naked little girl. Her back was bare and slim; her arms were folded across her breasts. She sat straddling a man who might have been dead or asleep; I never looked at his face because I was startled by the sight of the pale, delicate body that didn't seem to belong in that room or in the house.

There was something about her posture that suggested she'd been amused but was now bored, and she leaned back, still keeping her arms crossed over her breasts. I should have recognized her shoulder bones.

I stood in the doorway, transfixed and faint and afraid.

Suddenly she turned her head sharply and stared straight at me.

The room was dark, but there was moonlight through the window and I saw that it wasn't a child, but Justine. Her hair was now striped with streaks of red and gold, but her face was the same, fragile and doll-like, with her eyes pale blue and her lips red and sly.

I know I must have looked silly with gratitude because I was so stupidly happy. There she was, so I hadn't dreamt her up, so she wasn't dead, so I'd found her after all. And I could see why

I'd followed her the first time. You could just tell that she knew the Secret, that she'd done all kinds of things and never been defeated or ruined.

I didn't have to smile at her, though I did. She smiled back at me, and something passed between us. *Wait for me*, her eyes said. *I'll meet you in the hall.* Whatever passed between us then, I cannot name, but I bet it's the same thing that passes between spies who recognize each other, who are so grateful to be seen at last by someone who knows the truth behind the disguise.

THE cop is here. The cop is back.

He just barged in when I was in the bathroom, washing dirt off my hands.

Lucky for me, speed has killed off my guilty girl's lethargy.

I've been busy. He has no clue.

I've been hiding evidence; I'm no fool. I shoved Justine's records and books under my mattress. Her dresses are under my pillows. And in the garden, I buried the knife.

Deep down in the dirt, I buried the bloodied blade by the rosebush. My father will never go there for the rest of my life. The roots of roses will be strangled by my weapon: my weed, my bad seed.

I come out of the bathroom. I can't look him in the eye.

The cop says he has new information. Damaging New Information which Provides the Grounds to Arrest Me.

Could they have caught Justine? No. No, I know they haven't got her in handcuffs. He'd be gloating. Besides, I know they'll never find Justine. Look how long it took me.

"What's the new information?" I say. Then I pull my hair over my eyes.

"Why don't you just tell me what you did on Friday night?"

Yeah, right.

"Sara, you're not a bad person. I know you want to cooperate."

"I was so smashed. I don't remember anything about Friday night."

"I would think this incident is something you'd never forget."

"Think what you want. I drank a whole bottle of Aquavit."

I was wasted, wasted on white liquor and black beauties.

"I told you before I have a fever. Really, I'm not feeling well. I'm going to faint."

I walk right by him, head for my bedroom. He may be a cop, but he's still thirty. He can't infiltrate a girl's bedroom.

Lying down in my bed, I can still hear my heart, and my nose has started to bleed. My mouth's so dry. I wish I had some morphine. Wish I hadn't flushed away all my speed.

He just struts in. Stands with his legs apart, his hands on his hips, staring at my dresser like he's dead-set on discovering a girl's dirty diary.

Soon he'll say the word. It's hovering in his eyes; it's lingering on his lips.

"This is serious," he says. "This isn't shoplifting. This is—"

Call it tragic. Call it an *accident*. Just don't say the word *murder*, here, in my bedroom.

*   *   *

The cop says: *There are shadows in the spring and blossoms at the asylum and firs in the hands of boys who press plants down into charcoal that was once roots.*

No, he says: "Sara, we now know you were in possession of a knife."

He walks toward my bed.

He says: "We also know you were with Justine on Friday night."

That's right, I was. But I'll never say her name to this man.

I close my eyes and try to think of the pale petals on the Chinese emperor's trees. Some beauty that will still my heart and take away the fear that's floating over me.

I hear him breathe. He must be on his knees now; he must be praying like he's in the house of the holy.

I lift his hand so he can feel the heat inside me. He tries to take his hand away, but I won't let him. I want him to touch me where I'm warm. I want him to touch me there.

"Maybe you were just a witness, Sara. Just tell me if you're innocent."

Innocent, he says, this cop.

Innocent, I say. I am.

"Sara, I know. I know. You couldn't have done this. You're so—"

Now, he's leaning over me, touching my forehead.

His palm is soft with a sick girl's sweat. Sadly, he says, "You're so innocent."

I let his lips kiss mine. 'Cause when he tastes my fever, he'll believe I'm true.

No, he doesn't kiss me.

He says, "Shit," and jumps back from my bed, startled by the sudden roar of a thundering knock on the front door.

*   *   *

At first, I think it's my father. Thank God, Seamus, he's returned.

Then I realize he wouldn't knock and I think it's a SWAT team. I swear. I saw one on a TV screen when I was a little girl and my mom was watching the capture of Patty Hearst: masked men with their long black guns, an army in camouflage.

The cop turns his back on me. Tugs his pants as he walks away from my bed.

I bet he's not thinking about ice water or morphine. He's got his report; his pager; his siren; his gun. His sterling rep, his paycheck.

It's not a SWAT team, of course. It's not Everly. It's not Justine. It's not Glinda the Good Witch or Florence Nightingale.

It's another cop, who strides into my bedroom with a search warrant. He's pockmarked and pissed off; he's probably a prodigy or whatever it's called when you're good at pushing people into walls.

He calls me Miss. As in *Are you Ready to Go, Miss Shaw?*

"She has a fever. I don't know if we can bring her in."

"Yeah," I announce, "I'm quite ill."

It's creepy, the language of police. I can hear them whispering by my desk. *Did she give it up? Did she give you anything? No, she didn't give me anything.*

"Where's her dad?"

"He's on his way from Tofino. He was supposed to be here by now."

The new cop shakes his head. Crazy Hippie. No Wonder. I bet they'll seize his dead weed.

"Well, Miss Shaw, would you like a lawyer?"

As if I'm gonna ask for a lawyer! That's just like admitting you have something to hide.

"No, I don't need a lawyer."

"Well, you're still going to have to get out of bed."

"But my dad—"

"You're going to have to come down to the station with us."

"What for? I already told him I don't remember—"

"You're under arrest."

Under arrest. And that's how it feels too, when they snap cold metal bracelets on your wrists because you're a former runaway with violent tendencies. That's how it feels when they make you sit in the backseat of their cruiser, and you press your face against the leather warmed by the ass of their last criminal. That's how it feels when you won't look out the window because you don't want your neighbor to see. You're staring at the walkie-talkie blaring a staticky cop code you're not meant to understand.

It's like you're being pushed below the place where you used to stand and you know you're not likely to resurface.

Underwater, underground, they may as well have used those words because, really, *underwater, underground, under arrest*—there's really no difference.

*   *   *

Then they put me in this room. It smells like Big Macs and baby powder in here. Dr. Seuss books are scattered all over the floor. Cartoon stories defaced by crayon drawings of gorillas and burning homes.

I don't really know why the cops put me in the kiddie room.

When they brought me to the police station, they took my photo and made me sign some forms and then they put me in this room with the teddy bears.

"This whole thing must be very frightening for you," the

woman detective says. "You're a young girl, this must be over-whelming." I bet they think she will be the one to get me to talk about Friday night: a pregnant woman, all pink-skinned and motherly.

She takes away my clothes. So now, I'm dressed in a sleeveless smock. It's pale blue, paper thin.

I put my hand on the hem of the smock, trying my best to pull it down.

When my fever returns, my skin will melt this criminal costume away.

*   *   *

My lawyer better get here soon. I picked him out of the phone book because I liked his name. Edmundo Horatio.

I've never met a lawyer in my life. Maybe he'll be like that father guy on Dynasty, silver-haired and so serene. When he arrives, I have to be less sullen and sulky. I can't fuck it up with Mr. Horatio. I will tell him I'm not sleazy or sordid, though it probably looks that way. I practice saying it, under my breath: I'm a good person. I'm a good person. I am.

But really, I wish my lawyer could be Lemmy. Why are the people who would understand you, why are they far away, just faces on record covers and magazines?

Lemmy would understand. He would say: I know you're not a bad person. Sara, I know you never meant to be there with the blood and the screams and the knife and the blood and the screams and the knife in the alley.

*   *   *

There was rain on the streets. Her black dress slipped off her shoulders and there was rain on her shoulders. She shivered and she said she was always cold. Rain on her shoulders. I gave her China's coat, and the knife slipped from the white fur and lay in the grass, all silvery and daggerlike. I don't remember anything else. There were lilies on the lake, floating like nervous angels. Look, Justine said, pointing at the little man-made lake. See the swan? That's right where I was when I was stolen.

I saw the long curve of the neck, and the white wings, lifting. Then the swan was moving over the white floating flowers, and I felt this strange sadness in my chest.

*   *   *

I know how they try to trick you. China told me. First, they busted her when she was wasted. Then, they interrogated her till she was dizzy and shaky with shame. Trick questions, she said, that's what those assholes use. *When did you first fall in love? When did you lose your virginity?*

Well, no one's tricking me. They tried. When I was in the back-seat of the cruiser, and again, when they sicced the future mother on me. *Sara, we know you were in White Oaks. We know you have violent tendencies. Just tell us who held the knife. Tell us why you were feeling so angry.*

I just said the same answer, over and over, till I started to believe it was true. *I have nothing to say.*

I have nothing to say. Go away.

*   *   *

I think it might be dark outside. Maybe it's as dark as the night I found Justine. After we left the Blue House, every empty street was shining and the pavement tilted. I looked up and the moon was swaying and the stars seemed to be staggering. The whole world seemed drunk and I liked it that way.

*   *   *

Edmundo is not what I expected. There's no silver in his hair. He's around thirty-five, with a scraggly beard, and he's wearing a *sweatshirt* and khaki shorts and wool socks with his Birkenstocks. He could be one of those hiker guys who came to my dad's restaurant for the health food. Can I change my mind? Oh God, please. He's probably a pothead. He could never understand the images starting to come back to me. No, this guy could never understand the images of the streets and the knife and her thin, restless roving body.

"OK," he says. "You haven't said anything, good. No right to detain you or interview you without an adult—egregious abuse of rights. You're shivering, I'll get you a blanket. No fingerprints, right. No weapon. They've got nothing. You don't know where the knife is, I heard you the first time. Don't protest too much. Doesn't look good. They've got nothing. So I'm *suggesting* this, Sara. I'm *suggesting* the other girl—who by the way is known to the police as a person of bad character with a severe case of antisocial disorder—I'm suggesting this other girl was the main perpetrator. Unfortunately, ahem, this other girl has not been found. Perhaps, I'm guessing, she has a certain allure. I'm *suggesting*, you were under her sway. Are you the gullible type? Are you easily deceived? Impressionable? No problemo. We'll get some witnesses who can testify to that. You'd been drinking . . . your faculties were, shall we say, impaired. Look, I know you kids can get into trouble. You're what, just barely sixteen? Pshaw. A babe in the woods. Happens all the time. I don't like this one witness. He said he only met you once, and he's pretty damn vague. I'll destroy him. Sleazy character. No jury's gonna like him. I'll *destroy* him. He's going down. Well, your father, he's not exactly the perfect role model, is he? Your mother, can I get hold of her? Sorry I'm talking so fast do you understand what I'm saying let's just close our eyes and pray that this poor fellow pulls out of it because hold on a minute here sergeant we're talking can't you see."

*   *   *

He's gone to talk to the cops. I just want to sleep but they leave the lights on and there's no bed in the kiddie room and maybe I'll never sleep again. No rest for the wicked. So, he wants me to blame it on Justine. *I'm suggesting the other girl was the main perpetrator.* What none of these guys would believe is that she was trying to protect me. They'll laugh. Even the pregnant woman. She'll say, *She didn't even know you, Sara.* But she did. Know me, I mean. She did.

When Justine came out of the bedroom, she touched my forehead and asked me if I was feeling OK, and I realized no one had ever asked me that before.

Images of those minutes race in my mind, but I try to push them all away so I can lie more honestly. I'm guilty of something, that's for sure. I just don't know what it's called.

Images come rushing when I close my eyes. The knife in the grass, her legs lifting as she ran.

They come rapid-fire, and won't fade to gray. And the rest of the time, I'm being read my rights. I'm being told that it's a crime to obstruct justice by giving a false statement and I'm being asked about my whereabouts and asked if I have hate in my heart and I'm being told that I should understand the seriousness and consequences of not telling the truth.

They can yell at me all they want, but there are things I will never tell the cops. I stay quiet; I drink water; I touch the paper cloth.

*   *   *

In the bathroom, I'm not looking in the mirror. Never ever never want to see my face again.

The bathroom smells like cats and dust. The chemical sadness from crashing off speed; that aftertaste of bile, the tongue like Styrofoam. The bathroom scent reminds me of this girl Gaia; she used to be my friend in Oregon. She found wild kitties in the fields and kept them hidden in rough, gold hay. I wonder where she is now; she's probably a vet and has a farmer boyfriend who loves her because she's so devoted to the animal race.

The pregnant detective probably thinks I keep hiding in the bathroom because I'm petrified.

But really, I just want to press my cheek on the white tiles. I'm trying to remember how China did it. When we were in the bathroom of the Day and Night. She sprawled, she spat; she drank perfume. Anyone could have seen she didn't give a fuck and she wasn't afraid, not even deep down inside and secretly.

*   *   *

When I walk out of the bathroom, I see my dad. His scalp's sunburned, stubble covers his cheeks and chin. Standing by the detectives, I don't know why, but he has never looked so small and weak and kind.

"Attempted murder," he's screaming, "don't feed me this bullshit."

My poor father, they found him in Eden and told him of his daughter's crime.

But he doesn't yell at me when he comes into the kiddie room. He hugs me, and I bury my face in his flannel and breathe in the smell of firesmoke and pinecones. My dad's the only man who will ever see me cry.

"I'm sorry," I tell him, but he's not listening.

"Honey, don't let them break you," he says. "This is a farce. I mean, a farce! Darling, I'll get you out of here. We'll go back to the forest. You're so brave, handling this on your own. It's going to be OK. I'll take care of everything. And when you're ready to talk about it, you know I'm here and I'll understand. Don't think I haven't heard worse. I saw my buddies come back shell-shocked from the war. Riots in the streets of Portland. Hell's Angels armed and wired shoving shotguns in my face. The FBI have me on file I'm sure they're swapping—

"What? Yes, you were born with a fever. Yes, it lasted for three days. Don't know why. You just came out of the womb burning, that's what your mother used to say. The doula said it was dangerous. The doctors told us abnormal neuroblastomas. But we said, 'Fever's a sign that our daughter's not like all the others, that she's blessed.' And you are, Sara. You're so special, whatever these assassins tell you. You're fighting too hard and feeling too much. Honey, you look so wan and tired. They've kept you up all night and they'll just keep trying to break you. That's what the state's henchmen do.

"Listen to me, I understand, all crime springs from some necessity.

"I know that, I understand. But, this is very serious and your whole life's at stake. God, you look exhausted. Hey, you fuckers. Why don't you let my daughter get some sleep?"

*   *   *

When he's gone, they say I can sleep. After a few more questions. Go ahead. I stare down at the blue cloth of my paper dress, keep my hands on my bruised knees. The camera will capture this: my eyelids, instead of my pupils. My lips closed like when I was back in school and I knew I would be liked better if I just stayed mute. Here we go. Again. They press the Record button on their dinky tape deck.

"Did you know the vic— Dirk Wallace?"

"No."

"Did he provoke you in any way?"

"What does that mean?"

"Did he *provoke* you—did he call you names?"

"Yeah, he called me a bitch."

"Now why would he do that? He's never met you before."

I shouldn't have started talking because I haven't before. I know they want to get me on more than attempted. They want to get me on premeditated, first-degree. They've read my notebook. I can see. They've read my words. *Remove her enemy.*

"I'd just seen him around."

"Where?"

"Just on some street somewhere. I don't really remember."

"A man calls you a bitch and you don't remember? That seems like something you'd never forget."

"Sara, don't you remember any details?"

"What was he wearing?"

"What time of day was it?"

Imagine if I told these guys. It was around midnight when his body lay under me and China moved her mouth and there was no longer music; there was no more Motörhead.

"Why do you think he spoke to you?"

"I don't know. Ask him."

"We'd love to. He's not in the most verbal condition. As I'm sure you understand. Now, look. Stop being so vague. Because we're trying to help you here, and this new information is helpful. He insulted you. You were upset. Maybe you were afraid? That's understandable. So you're upset with him and you're afraid and so you tell your friend Justine, who's a bit of a hothead and—"

"No. She's—"

"Let's not talk about her. Because you get upset every time we bring her up. Let's leave her out of this for now. So, Mr. Wallace, he's just strolling down the street and he calls you a bitch. Something's missing there, don't you think?"

"Can I have some water please—"

"Sara, I'm gonna tell you something. Honestly. Me and my partner, we both like you. We've dealt with Justine numerous times, and she's a handful. But you're a nice girl. Really. We think you are. You were starting to talk just now, and that's good. It must feel good, huh? To get this off your chest. You're all alone with what happened. You don't have anyone. We understand. You're a young girl and you're scared. This must have been something you never wanted to happen. Right?"

"I'm so hot right now could I—"

"And, you're going to be talking to a lot of people. Maybe a judge. Maybe a jury. And I got to tell you, everyone is going to want to hear a story that makes sense. Not stuff about how you have a fever. I've got athlete's foot, you know, my partner here has allergies. No one cares! When a man's been stabbed in the heart, no one cares. They want Facts. So, give me a date."

"I don't remember. I think it was the day before I dropped out of school."

"That would be May twenty-eighth, when you were *asked to leave* school. But—never mind. Good. That's a fact. A date. Now, help me out here with the logic. I mean, what logical reason would Mr. Wallace have for calling you a bitch?"

"He was just in a bad mood? I don't know."

"Did he know you?"

"No. He didn't know me at all."

"Well, I find this hard to believe. Why would a man like Mr. Wallace even talk to you?"

"Because he knew my friend."

Oops.

"What friend?"

"Ch— Alice."

"Chalice?"

"Yeah."

"Who is she?"

"She's a— She's—"

"A what?"

"She's just a girl I knew."

"And where is she now?"

"I don't want her involved."

"Well, she *is* involved. You just told us her name! I'm sure she would want to help you out. And, to be honest, you *need* someone to back up your story, because you're looking like a liar right now."

"But she's gone."

"Gone where?"

"I don't know. I thought you were going to take my temperature."

"We've taken your temperature three times and you're normal. You're perfectly fine. Now, stop jerking my chain. Look at me. Sara, look at me. *Where is Chalice?*"

"She's at the school for maps."

"*The school for maps?* OK. Gotcha. Let's wrap this up. Interview

over. June eighth. 2:35 A.M. File case 84-28976. Anything
you'd like to add?"

Yeah, fuck off.

"No."

*   *   *

It gets hard, faking like you don't care. Only I don't care. I don't
give a fuck. I hate you all. I hate your guts.

Only. Only. Only.

Only I wish I had someone to ask for advice. Cassie, Amber, I
wish I could give them a call. Hey girls, they've got me for
something I didn't really do.

I keep trying to think of the words to say 'cause it's not so
easy though everyone thinks it is. So simple. Say something. Say
nothing. Call it evil. Call it a mistake. Blame it on him, blame it
on your best friend, blame it on the Aquavit.

It's got me confused.

*Dear Abby, Dear Everly, Dear Lemmy, just come and hold me and tell me
what I should do.*

It's got me scared.

But no, I don't give a fuck.

Throw me in jail, call me Victoria's first teen girl murderess.

*   *   *

Cheryl, the future mother, brings me a pillow and blanket. She
doesn't want me to sleep in the dungeon. City cells, they're
called, the cells in the basement of the station. She says I can
catch a little shut-eye in the kiddie room.

That's what she says. *Catch a little shut-eye.*

"Thanks," I say, because she smiles in this sympathetic way when she hands me the blanket, like she knows how it feels to stay awake talking when you just want to be silent and dream. I don't really know what to say to her. I take the blanket and hold it near my chest gratefully. "Thanks," I say and I take the blanket and hold it near my chest.

I have this mad urge to ask her if she's chosen her child's name.

For a moment, she lingers, like maybe she's considering singing me a lullaby. Then, she pats her stomach, and leaves me here in the dark room.

I try to sleep, but I'm afraid of what I'll dream. Myself, in white, and Justine, in black, crossing the forbidden border, into the Red Zone.

Let's go home, I said, but the word made her cringe.

I don't go home.

The thin girl in a black dress whirling around in the bar of the King's Hotel.

Dirk, with his flannel shirt, sleeves rolled up.

You owe me something.

There are hopeless shadows in this room at the police station; there are shadows that menace and move, shadows like sickles and serpentines.

Justine slithered under the Dumpster; she wanted to give me a gift.

I put the pillow over my face, pull the blanket over my head, and close my eyes. If I sleep, I want to dream of her gift. Covered in gravel, the dirty paperback of her famous father's poetry.

*   *   *

"Now, Sara," Edmundo says, as if he's talking to a retarded child. "Now, Sara, the police have prepared a report on you.

The report is with the Crown, and that's the government, OK? The Crown will tell the Judge what you should be charged with because you've been arrested, but you haven't been charged yet. OK? Are you following me?"

Edmundo is wearing a T-shirt that has a drawing of a sailboat and then above the sailboat it says Tommy's Last Sail, and I guess it's some memento from his best friend's bachelor party.

"Now, you have the right to read this report."

"Is it about Justine?"

"No, it's about you," he says, and there it is, my name typed officially.

SARA SHAW. File case 84-28976.

The following is a report relating to the suspect SARA SHAW's role in the incident on the person of Dirk Wallace on the evening of June 5.

Detectives Haywood and Vowell have conducted four interviews with detained suspect. On all four occasions, she has been reluctant and resistant to provide information.

On June 5, she admits to being present at a party "somewhere in Fairfield." On the exact address of her location, she is unclear. During the course of the party, the suspect met JUSTINE K. Suspect states that immediately after meeting Justine, she "blacked out." In further interviews, she states she had a "fever." She also states she has "a fucked-up memory."

The suspect thus provides no details as to the incident which occurred in the alley between Yates and Pandora Street at approximately 2:35 A.M.

*   *   *

The following is a preliminary synopsis of information homicide detectives have gathered in regard to Shaw:

On June 5, Shaw was at 1345 Bramley Crescent in Fairfield. Location is a known "party house" rented by LUCE TATHERS, a known heroin dealer and harborer of Red Zoned youth.

Shaw was intoxicated on alcohol, amphetamines, and possibly heroin.

According to witnesses, she was "falling all over the place . . . making out with some guy . . . being really obnoxious." Heroin use was rampant, and "she seemed really fascinated by all the junkies."

Statements from witnesses LILY LESAGE and CHARMAINE CAMPBELL are enclosed.

Shaw <u>did not</u> black out but, in fact, left the premises with Justine K. at approximately 12:15.

"They were holding hands and whispering." Lesage is very clear on the time of 12:15: "I remember thinking they were my little sister's age and she would never be out so late because she has an 11:00 curfew."

Lesage and Campbell came to the police on their own wherewithal after hearing of the attack on CHEK-TV. "When the reporter said it was supposedly two teenage girls, we just had this chilly feeling and we knew it was those two."

They proceeded to correctly identify both suspects from photo ID lineup.

Note: Lesage and Campbell are willing to testify. They are 21-year-old theater students at the University of Victoria. We find them highly credible and of good character.

At approximately 2:00, the two enter the premises of the King's Hotel. We find it noteworthy and a potential additional felony under Section 126 that Shaw failed to provide an account of the following event:

The bar was closing, and ROADHOUSE (MARK KLASSEN), the bartender, was approached by Justine K. She demanded a six-pack and said it was not for her but an adult friend. Klassen informed her that he could not serve or sell to a minor. He has had numerous dealings with K. in the past as she often sneaks into the bar and "flirts with old men and tries to get a rise out of loggers. She just likes to start shit." When he refused to sell her off-sales, "Justine got really belligerent, like she always does. She also screamed that she was not a minor, but a major." Klassen states that he informed the proprietor, HEINRICH GUNTHER, that the "tiny terror" was on the premises and to alert the police because "I couldn't handle her. She was out of control." He briefly glimpsed Shaw and noticed that "she was laughing . . . she seemed to be getting a kick out of the whole scene. She looked vaguely familiar, but I can't be sure that I've ever seen her before."

Klassen prefers not to testify because "Gunther doesn't want our bar to get a bad rep."

CAL CODY, a temporarily unemployed forestry worker, states that he saw "a pretty girl in a white fur coat and tight white dress . . . like a nurse's uniform. She was leaning on the doorway, kind of slumped, like she had the spins, and I was going to go see if she needed help, when all of a sudden she got this frightened look and she just bails. I thought she saw her dad, 'cause she had that look, like 'Oh shit, I'm gonna get a whupping.'"

Cody prefers not to testify because "I was pretty hammered and I don't want to have a bunch of fucking lawyers asking me how much I drank." Cody is not a credible witness as he has three prior charges of drunk and disorderly and was drunk during the course of his police interview.

At 2:15, the bar in the King's Hotel closed. STANLEY SMOTHERS left the bar and proceeded to the Douglas Street parkade. Car is a 1979 Cadillac. License plate BTR-519. Videotape provided by Kinney confirms said car was in parkade at said time. At this time, he saw "two girls run into the alley like they were running for something." He did not see the victim at this time.

At 2:35 approximately, Smothers exited the parkade and proceeded to drive down Yates Street. It was at this time that he saw the taller girl, in white, running and <u>alone</u>.

Smothers is certain that this girl was by herself.

Smothers slowed down and attempted to ask the girl if she needed a drive. It was at this point that he recognized her as a girl "Sara" whom he had met before.

"I noticed she was a girl I'd met before, and I noticed she was carrying a suitcase. I was concerned for her being alone on the street at that hour." Smothers felt the suspect deliberately evaded him after he honked his horn. "She just ran away from me and disappeared. At the time, I thought she was treating me as if I was scum.

You know, I thought, I'm trying to help you. No need to be rude."

Smothers noticed no blood. "I wasn't checking out her body. She could have been covered in blood."

The next evening, Smothers returned to the King's Hotel, where he was informed by friends that police were asking about a stabbing incident in the alley. Smothers immediately contacted police and informed us about seeing a girl enter and later leave the alley at said time on said evening.

Note: Smothers is a freelance photographer for a modeling agency. He states that he met suspect on May 27, at the Day and Night diner on Yates Street. She approached him and his friend, a modeling scout, and expressed an interest in a modeling career.

When asked if Smothers's eyewitness account was accurate, Shaw provided no answer. When asked if she had, in fact, met him previously at a diner, she mumbled. While transcriber has typed this mumble as "illegible," Vowell noted her words were: "That fucking pervert."

Note: Smothers is willing to testify. He identified Shaw from a photo ID lineup in less than two seconds. We find him to be credible and of good character.

Based on Smothers's tip, Detective Haywood proceeded to investigate the identity of a formerly red-haired 16-year-old girl named Sara. A contact in the Social Services office was able to provide him with address and last name. Contact would like to remain anonymous at this time.

On June 7, at 11:35 A.M., Haywood went to the Shaw residence at ▉▉▉▉▉▉. He found a girl matching the descriptions provided by Lesage: "Dyed white hair with red roots, around 5'8, pale. " Also matched the description of Smothers: "High forehead, freckles under her eyes, no makeup, tendency to slouch and frown."

Suspect acknowledged that her name was Sara and she was 16 years old.

However, her demeanor was evasive, and she was alternately shy and hostile. She refused to provide information on the whereabouts of her mother or father. When he asked if they could have a chat, she told him she had "a fever" and he "better stay away."

She then stated that she was going into her bedroom, and feeling that an interview in the bedroom of a minor female would be improper, Haywood immediately left the premises. He maintained surveillance. At 1:38, the suspect pulled back the curtain of her bedroom window and gave him the finger. That was their only contact until 4:33.

At that time, he received a radio call from Detective CHERYL BARTON. She informed him that on May 28, Shaw attempted to stab a fellow student at Mount Douglas Senior Secondary during an afternoon pep rally.

On June 1, Shaw was found passed out in the bathroom of LE GARDIN restaurant after attempting to vandalize the bathroom. At that time, she was brought to WHITE OAKS Shelter. While there, she informed ELAINE COLLINS that she should not be put in a foster home because she had "violent tendencies, violent urges, violent dreams."

Detective Haywood was informed by investigation supervisor that he should immediately enter the premises and conduct further questioning and observation. He immediately did so.

Again, Shaw behaved in a suspicious manner and

referred repeatedly to her "fever." At the time, Haywood felt that Shaw was covering up for—and possibly in fear of—Justine K. He encouraged her to tell him if she was innocent. She responded, "Innocent. I am." But she provided no further information as to what occurred in the Yates Street alley.

Note: Haywood has investigated 44 serious crimes and has not once dealt with a teenage girl. He admits that he was "awkward" and "disturbed" and felt "protective" toward the young girl as she was alone and without any adult supervision. The unusual situation accounts for his failure to record the conversation that took place in the kitchen of the Shaw home. No handwritten notes exist.

At 4:48, Detective Vowell entered the Shaw home and executed search warrant. He noted suspect was "extremely pale . . . shaky . . . dilated pupils . . . signs of amphetamine influence . . . pulling her hair over face and would not make eye contact."

Haywood escorted Shaw to his vehicle. She did not resist.

Vowell undertook search of bedroom.

He found dresses under the pillow, records and books under the mattress, and a suitcase under the bed. He seized these items, which are believed to have belonged to Justine K.

Suspect becomes particularly distressed when asked to explain how Justine K.'s possessions ended up in her bedroom.

A white dress/uniform with torn hem was also seized. Material appears identical to torn piece of white cloth found in victim's wound.

Clothing is currently under analysis at crime lab.

Writings by both accused are enclosed and may provide motive as well as attest to violent and antisocial tendencies on part of both accused. Of particular note is Shaw's jotting "FTW," which is juvenile slang for "Fuck the World." She has also written, "Fever is nature's engine which she brings into the field to remove her enemy." The words "remove her enemy" have been heavily underlined.

Executed search warrant also produced a Polaroid photo. Said photo appears to have been taken in the vicinity of the Royal Victoria Wax Museum. Shaw has her arm around unidentified girl in tan raincoat. Unidentified girl appears to match photos of "TAHITI" (last name unknown), who is known to the police and has two prior records for solicitation for the purposes of prostitution. When asked who the girl in the Polaroid is, Shaw denied knowledge of minor prostitute named Tahiti. Whereabouts of "Tahiti" are currently unknown.

Of note is that Polaroid shows Shaw clearly brandishing a Victorinox knife with an extracted blade. The knife is in her left hand, and she is smiling broadly. The knife matches the description provided by Mount Douglas Principal DAVE LOCKE. We find Principal Locke credible, and he will testify.

Photo and corroboratory eyewitness evidence verify Shaw was owner of knife.

Further analysis and medical reports could verify that said knife was weapon used in attack on the person of Dirk Wallace.

When asked if she owned a knife, she replied, "My

dad gave me a Swiss Army knife for my birthday when I turned fourteen." It is of note that the wounds sustained by victim could not credibly have been inflicted by a Swiss Army knife.

Last, in regard to the victim, Shaw initially said she "doesn't know the guy." Upon further questioning, she however stated that victim Wallace called her "a bitch" on some street somewhere when she was with a girl named "Chalice," who is now at "a school for maps." Detectives are unable to find any records for a girl named "Chalice." No "schools for maps" exist in British Columbia.

However, if the bitch incident can be verified, Shaw has reason for <u>animus</u> toward the victim. Insult also provides <u>motive</u> to harm his person.

Victim Dirk Wallace entered Royal Jubilee Hospital at 2:55 A.M. He was placed in critical ward with life-threatening injuries.

Victim Dirk Wallace is currently under heavy sedation and unable to provide identification or statement. He is a 43-year-old married father of two daughters, a newborn of three months and a 6-year-old. He is employed by WHITE WATER TOURS as a sales representative. His coworker JEFF MALIN has provided statement to the effect that Mr. Wallace often drank at the King's Hotel and on the Friday night in question was probably "celebrating payday." Mr. Wallace has no criminal record. He has had numerous calls of support and concern from a wide range of respected members of the tourist industry and whale-watching community.

*   *   *

It looks so bad.

All this time I thought they had no idea and fuck off and die 'cause the joke's on me.

Cheer up, Edmundo says. *Cheer up.* Lemmy wouldn't say cheer up after giving me this report to read. He'd say, *Let's snort a line, let's get some brass knuckles, let's start a war.*

"They've got all these facts and—"

"It's just circumstantial, Sara, it doesn't prove a thing. They have no evidence that you stabbed this fellow—"

"But they know I had a knife. They have a picture!"

"You were a young girl alone on the streets. You had a knife, so what? It's a scary world, right?"

It's really getting to me that he's not more upset by their words.

"Can I have a glass of water?"

"Sara, I've brought you twenty-five glasses. You're drinking this place dry."

"Do you think they'll find that girl in the Polaroid, 'cause I don't want her involved."

"Police have better things to do than chase down teenage runaways. You know what they call girls like Justine? They call them Bic lighters."

"What's that supposed to mean?"

"Bic lighters, you know, disposable."

"She's not a Bic lighter!"

"Look, Sara, stop worrying about other girls. Worry about yourself."

I look back at their words, and it feels like every one of those dates and names and times is a tentacle threatening to strangle me.

I should just confess. I should. Just tell the judge what really happened 'cause they've got it so wrong.

I tell Edmundo I want to confess.

He says that's dumb. Just dumb.

He *suggests* I keep my mouth shut. I'll only get myself in more trouble if I talk. He *advises* me to just let him do the talking.

But how can he talk for me? Maybe if I wrote a report, I could make the judge understand because my words would smell like cigarettes and perfume. They wouldn't be so dead and false and untrue.

"I want to write—"

"I'm meeting with the judge in half an hour."

"Can't I just write what really happened, 'cause it's a long story and I have a lot to—"

"Listen to me, Sara. I'll tell the judge they're scapegoating you because the police don't have any real evidence. Nada. Zilch. A couple of drunk losers saw you in the area, or so they say. She'll give you bail; she's a nice lady."

He says after I get bail, he'll take me to Red Lobster for dinner. "Cheer up," he says. "Smile," he says. "Stop looking so freaked out." He says, "You're a pretty girl when you smile, as I'm sure lots of people have told you before."

"Yeah, just get me a pen," I tell him, and I pull my hair over my eyes so he won't see the tears.

Edmundo gives me a new notebook.

It's funny because, as soon as I have the notebook, I do, for the first time, want to write it all down. Just to understand. Just to figure out, for myself, what happened in that alley. There's only a few details missing, and those details matter to me. A man, stabbed in the heart, don't think I don't care.

They need to know. It's only fair.

You probably think I'm guilty. A heart full of hate. You're like the rest of them. You think I wanted him to die. But it wasn't like that at all. Really, it wasn't like that at all.

I start to write: I first saw Justine at Ming's.

But that's not *relevant*, I know.

So I erase those words. I erase I first saw Justine at Ming's.

The pencil is comforting, just holding it in my hand.

I consider, my thoughts, my frail fucked-up memory.

I write: On the evening of the 5th, I entered the premises on Bramley Crescent on my own recognizance. I proceeded toward a state of severe intoxication.

Then I erase that too.

*   *   *

Maybe it was midnight when she came out of the bedroom, thin and delicate and slipping a black lace dress over her pale, naked body. The wrinkled dress might have been made for a widow, but Justine looked more like a drunk ballerina than a woman heading for a funeral.

She turned suddenly, and came right up to me. I tried not to stare at her, but it was impossible. A strand of hacked black hair covered her blue eye; her mascara smeared, her small face so ivory and delicate and haunted, slightly.

How do you like my dress? she said, in a way that was completely innocent, but seemed slightly taunting, like I was being asked to play truth or dare.

It's nice, I stuttered.

Nice? It's lascivious. It's posh. I like it, she said, and she touched the black cloth, rubbing her hand from her thigh to her hips.

Then her tiny hand darted out and touched the stiff white cloth of my uniform.

I like yours, she said. Are you a nurse?

Kind of, I said. I'm in training, I guess.

As if she'd lost interest, she bent down, strapping on a pair of black stilettos with high, thin heels and crooked little leather bows. Taller now, she looked me right in the eye.

You're the girl from the floods, right? I saw them carrying you out of the restaurant. You were soaking wet, collapsed. I asked around. I have my sources. I found out all about how you were dying with a fever and so you started a flood to keep yourself alive.

Before we left that debauched house, Justine touched my forehead.

The best kind of nurse, she said, is a nurse with a malady.

I'd spent so much time in Nicholas's apartment; I forgot the thrill of being alone on the dark and empty streets. Something rose up in my heart; I felt myself soaring, as if I was suddenly winged. And Justine, even when she was walking, she seemed to be leaping. I just wanted to go wherever she went. I thought of that expression: If Justine jumped off a cliff, would you? And I thought, Yes, I would, *yes*.

Sirens and threats, the cops looking for her, Dirk Wallace wanting to bust up my face, none of that seemed real. The black streets and the black sky were tilting and swerving and the whole world seemed drunk and I liked it that way.

We wandered over gardens and lawns. We crept through hedges and ran by living rooms and we had no accidents and we didn't bother anyone.

*   *   *

She said she knew a guy with a thousand records. His house was always a party; he always let her DJ. Under the streets of Chinatown, she confessed, secret tunnels led to an opium den where a lady in a kimono passes around her pipe of poppies.

But we didn't end up at an opium den.

We ended up at the Lake for Forsaken Orphans.

We sat on a bench. The moon lit up the black wet circle. Lilies, I think they were lilies, some small white blossoms, floating flowers in murky, green leaves. There was a waterfall, and it was louder than my mother's water; it was loud and rushing, falling over the black rock, falling so fast the water was white.

In the mist, the lake and flowers seemed soft and blurred, and it reminded me of looking at something when you're crying, the way it wavers and hazes and almost fades away.

What is this place?, I asked Justine. Is it British?

It's Japanese, she said, in her way, so certain and sure.

She learned forward, elbows on her knees, her chin resting in her palm. I like to come here, she said, 'cause this is where I lost my dad.

She told me her story then. Not that it's your business, but just so you know, because it's not in that stupid police report.

She was a year old, bundled in blankets; her father was a poet. He brought her to the lake because he wanted to write a poem. He set her down for just one second. Just one second, he set me down and went off to his car to get a new pen. That's when she got stolen. Sara, she said, I was abducted by criminals. This sick, evil, lascivious couple.

They kept her in a basement, in blackness, and by the time the social workers found her, she'd learned to sing.

They said I was mute, but I wasn't mute. I'd just never

learned their words. They kept putting me in and out of foster homes, but I never forgot—

She leaned forward, further, staring at the lake.

Where's that swan? she said, and then she bit her lip.

She stood up, started walking toward the lake, and then suddenly turned, just as she had in the Blue House. She came back to me.

Where are you going? she demanded.

I don't know, home, I guess.

No, I mean, with your life. 'Cause I'm going to Crete to find my dad. No one here knows him, but over in Europe, he's really famous. Do you want to come? We can hitchhike, over to England, and then we'll go to Crete.

Her plan sounded really possible, the way she said it: *Hitchhike over to England, and then we'll go to Crete.*

Everyone I knew—Ivy, China, even Dean—they had all left Victoria, and so, now, at last, I could leave too. Why not? I didn't really know anything about Europe, but I thought those Europeans had been in a lot of wars and could use my nursing expertise.

Look, she said, see that swan? That's right where I was when I was stolen.

I saw the long curve of the neck and the white wings, lifting. Then the swan was in the reeds, and I felt this strange sadness in my chest.

How are we going to leave? I said.

I know this old guy Barnett. He'll give us a drive to the ferry if I bring him some off-sales. I can always get off-sales at the King's.

I noticed she was shivering then. I'd never seen anyone shiver like her. The dress had slipped from her shoulders, and they were wet with rain.

Here, I said, handing her China's coat. She stroked the fur for a few seconds, but she didn't take the coat. I'm used to being cold, she said, I'm cold all the time.

Now, they keep asking me if I saw anything violent in her, but I really didn't. She just looked so cold, and when she held the fur coat to her chest, her neck rose out of the whiteness, slim as the swan's.

As we were leaving, I saw a sign rammed in the grass. FOUNTAIN LAKE, the sign said. So what. So she'd made up her own name. Why did it matter? I liked her name better than the one on their sign.

I thought, *What did it matter?* Forsaken was a better word than fountain. Her word was better than the word the world had chosen to display.

But if I told the cops where we were, they would say that there is no such place as the Lake of Forsaken Orphans, and we find it on no map, young lady.

I should tell the cops this: I saw the knife in the grass. It must have fallen when I handed her China's coat.

The knife was in the grass like a silver dagger, and should I tell the cops this: I saw her take the knife from the grass.

I thought, *Let her have it.* It can be an inheritance, a gift, an award for those who never ask for weaponry.

We crossed the forbidden border, into the Red Zone.

All I really remember is that she told me the cops were looking for her because she started a fire in her foster home. She sliced the knife through the chain around her neck and the toothbrush fell to the ground, the dirty toothbrush I'd once seen her suck like candy. She said she'd seen the knife before. Some girl named Tahiti showed it to her in the bathroom of Kwon Tung's.

What did you think of her? I asked, nervously.

Tahiti? She seemed pretty jaded.

Jaded: I didn't even know what the word meant. I thought it was the smooth green stone we sold at the tourist store.

Maybe she knew the word because her father sent her letters from places I've never been. Maybe that's why she didn't say all the words I was sick of: *suck* and *man* and *slut*. *Jeans* and *fur* and *fuck*. *Keggers* and *smokes* and *party on*.

I saw the blade in her hands, now glistening with rain. It looked like silver and tears.

She flicked the blade and stabbed the air, again and again. I had my first kiss tonight, she said, before you found me in that bedroom. Have you been in love yet?

Before I could answer, she thrust the blade forward as if she wanted to kill the sky.

We can go to my house, I said, remembering suddenly the floral sheets and the flowers on the family china and the pale petals on the lilac trees. I had this instinct that I should get her off the streets where everyone hated her. I wanted her safe, even though I wasn't the savior kind.

I would write my dad and tell him to come home. Seamus would cook her pancakes and she could sing for him and they could exchange stories about living life as a fugitive.

Let's go home, I said, but the word made her cringe.

I don't go *home*, she said. We're going to Greece. Come on!

I didn't argue. I couldn't argue with Justine. Her eyes with their delicate look, and her holding herself, and shivering and starting to run, run away from me.

I caught up with her, and we walked into the King's.

The barroom smelled like tires. Brawny men in black leather vests, mustached men in flannel shirts and cowboy hats, their faces red and swarthy and devilly.

But she just busted in there, strutting by all the drunk men playing pinball and shooting pool. All the drunk men stared, and there was a swarthy chorus of What the fuck is that What the fuck is that, and Justine just laughed and kept walking as if she was in a palace and heading for her raised and dazzling throne.

I wouldn't have missed that scene for anything.

It was like a movie I'd always wanted to see.

I leaned back against the doorway, watching to see what she would do next.

She pressed her body against the bar. I'd given her twenty dollars; she threw the money down.

The bartender shook his head; she ignored him. She put her arm around the bus driver drowning his sorrows at the bar. She whispered in his ear, took off his navy cap, and placed it crooked on her hair. He seemed like a nice guy, the bus driver; I think he even reached over and lifted her dress back to cover her naked shoulder. I thought he would probably want to help her leave this town.

The walls of the tavern spun.

I was laughing so hard I fell down on the floor. I lost my gravity.

Some biker told me I was too young to be at the King's and I should leave.

I raised my head to tell him to fuck off, and that's when I saw Dirk.

*   *   *

Edmundo, he doesn't knock. He just walks in and looks at the blank page on the notebook he's given me. "Five minutes," he says.

When he's gone again, I just stare at the police report. I draw a line through Lily Lesage's and Charmaine Campbell's names and above the words *theater students*, I write IDIOTS. It's not what I want to say. But this must be my fatal flaw. When I most want to get it together, I just fuck it up. I fuck it up so stupidly.

*   *   *

On Yates Street, Justine staggered up to me. Under the streetlight, she hugged me so hard I could feel her hipbones. Close to her, under the sick, stale glow, I saw a burn mark in her black cloth, a bruise on her neck. Her hands were empty, but I no longer cared about getting some guy to drive us to the ferry.

Dirk had looked so different in the King's. He was wearing a plaid shirt, with the sleeves rolled up high, like he was some muscly, macho logger. When the waitress touched his empty glass, he'd slapped her hand and glared at her like she was the original thief.

Look, I said, I've got to go home. I've got to take my medicine.

She said she wanted to go into the alley. She said she wanted to give me some gift.

So, we ran into the alley. There was no one around.

I just remember being in that alley and feeling something kicking up in my heart. My heart hurt as I looked at her.

She crawled across the concrete.

Hurry, I should have said.

She slithered catlike toward a green Dumpster. Her hand slid under the heavy green steel.

When she had her suitcase, she started to sing. I should have told her to be quiet, because she was singing my name. Her voice was the only sound in the dark alley, where there were shadows moving against bricks.

She sat on the concrete, cross-legged, and turned the pages of a book. As if we were somewhere safe. As if we were in a library.

Come on, I wanted to say, but I sat down beside her. When I saw you in Ming's, she said, I thought you were the kind of girl who—

I wanted to hear her, but I never did.

Because that's when we heard his voice five feet away in the darkness. A voice without a body; a voice I'll always hear, whether I make it to New York or rot in jail.

You owe me something, you little bitch. You owe me.

I grabbed her suitcase and started to run, but what I should have done was take her hand.

I thought she'd follow me, though she never had before.

I don't owe you anything, she said to him.

He must have— I don't know what he did.

I don't even know you, she said, so fuck off! Get lost! Leave us alone! Hey—

Her voice went quiet, and I heard his moan. I ran to the end of the alley and once I left the narrow passage the wide street was empty and still as a tomb.

I just kept running and I swear on the Bible I never saw anything after that.

No, that's not true.

I walked back to Justine and saw her, a black silhouette, standing over his body.

Dirk Wallace was slumped on the concrete, and she was standing over his body. She was standing over his body; he was slumped on the concrete.

The delicate look she'd always had in her eyes, that was gone. I turned away from her. Her eyes were dull and dark, as if I'd only dreamed them clear blue.

Hey, she said, hey, Sara. Let's go to that party!

*   *   *

"I've got to go," Edmundo says, "I can't be late for the judge."

Something else happened too, something else happened in the alley.

I did something too. I did something in the alley.

Maybe later I'll find the time to write the story of my crime. But why bother when my words aren't what they want? They want people of good character and dates and times and facts and blame.

I just write the word: Blame.

Blame it on Led Zeppelin. Invent a new crime and call it: inevitable. Blame it on *The Lord of the Flies*. Call it riot and revenge, ricochet and roulette.

Really, I write, I really don't fucking care.

*   *   *

Edmundo just grabbed the page, and he never said a word. My confession might have been his keys or his watch, something to shove in his suitcase.

But when he comes back, he says he's not impressed by my poetic bullshit. He's not impressed, the judge is not impressed. "Quite frankly, no one's impressed, Sara."

"I guess I'm not going to Red Lobster."

"No," he says, "unfortunately, you are not."

The judge decided that I should be remanded to the youth custody center because there is sufficient evidence and I pose a threat to the community and I do not have a responsible guardian and clearly, I clearly do not demonstrate remorse if I am writing poetic nonsense instead of a confession or an apology.

"Jail's not so bad," Edmundo says. "Cheer up."

No, he doesn't say anything. He just rolls his eyes when I ask if I can keep the notebook.

I'm pretty sure he wants to fire me.

I READ the newspaper article. The newspaper got it all wrong.

"Impressionable" and "troubled." They should have called me a harlot and a slut, a poseur and a tease, a nubile and naive, a slattern and a sleaze, a vandalist, an anarchist, a dirty dilettante with a fatal and fervent disease.

Because I was all those things in the twelve days when there was too much rain and I was burning and I found and lost Justine.

"Authorities say the incident was instigated by a streetwise, disturbed girl." Authorities say. Yeah, sure. That line always makes me laugh.

I shove the newspaper article under the mattress in my cell. My cell is painted gray and blue. Gray like the fog, blue like the ocean, the constant parts of my island I used to see every day, but no longer see now that I'm inside juvie.

I'm high up in the Sooke hills; fifteen miles from downtown, in a concrete slab surrounded by Christmas trees.

It's like being back in Mount Doug, with the fluorescent glare and the smell of Lysol everywhere. There's a cafeteria and classrooms and a basketball court. It's not like the jails you see on TV. There's no moat, no roaming dogs, no watchtower or barbed-wire fence.

At juvie, they frisked me as if my skin was contraband.

I'm high-risk, they said, I'm at risk.

*   *   *

The visitors' room is a laid-back place, with a beanbag chair and a pinball machine. There's a trophy case full of artwork from the former inmate kids—macramé baskets and clay rainbows.

Seamus is there, as often as they'll let him be. He's never high, even though I can tell he's in bad shape; his fingernails bitten away, his chin full of razor nicks. It must be the worst thing to have everyone think your daughter is a fuckup with violent tendencies, especially when you're a father who's never raised his voice, never says what I hear other parents scream: *How could you do this to me?*

My father says, *All crime springs from some necessity.*

He brought me the books I asked for. *Flowers for Hitler, Beautiful Losers.*

I tell my dad Justine's dad wrote those books.

"Oh *come on*," he says.

I don't tell my dad that in the moments before my bogeyman appeared, in Ming's and in the reeds and in the bedroom of the

Blue House, she moved just like you'd think a poet's daughter would, sly and certain, like she was too good for this dull world.

I read the back of his books. They say he's somewhere in Greece. I hope she's with him, on an island where the buildings are white stone instead of gray concrete, where the water's clear, not murky and heavy with seaweed. I hope she's with her father because he has her same smile, wry and kind.

"Oh come on," Seamus says. "Leonard Cohen is not her dad!"

*   *   *

My fellow criminals are kind to me. The people the world hates, they're the ones who understand. I'm not very friendly, but no one in juvie calls me the Ice Queen.

Maybe I belong here.

Maybe jail is where I belong after all. Maybe not, maybe.

Hey, they yell, when they walk past my cell, keep your head up, Sara! Be a fighter. Barry, a serial shoplifter, wants to give me a FUCK THE WORLD tattoo.

But outside, I'm despised. I'm villainous, vicious, vile, vilified.

CHEK-TV 6:00 news. Girl, 16, Arrested in Savage Attack. In the alley, carnations lie limply; little flames flicker from the candles. A hand-painted sign billows over the bricks: GET WELL SOON DIRK.

Man-on-the-street interviews, what a joke.

Question of the day: How do you feel about the vicious attack on Dirk Wallace?

Considering none of these people know what happened, they've sure got a lot to say.

This one old lady with blue-rinsed hair and a Picasso umbrella: "I do believe the Lord will have those girls burn in hell! The one that's missing, she's probably already there."

                              *   *   *

My new lawyer is a friend of my neighbor's. The man who gave us his secondhand technology took pity on us and said he'd pay to have me represented properly.

Or maybe Seamus caved in and called Everly. I like to believe she sent a check from Palm Springs. When you're locked up, you can have these hopes, or whatever the wanting of a secret savior is called—daydreams, delusion, a lost daughter's fantasy.

Anyway, I like my new lawyer so much more than that fool Edmundo. He's even better than the man on *Dynasty*. Mr. Galloway, he's probably around fifty; he looks wealthy and clean. He must live in a mansion in Uplands, maybe next door to that movie producer who was always in Los Angeles. I wonder if, nights, him and his wife hear the secret sound of boys skateboarding in an empty swimming pool.

He has wise eyes; he wears pin-striped suits.

I like his manner.

He never *suggests*. He just tells me that the police have a weak case based on what's called circumstantial evidence. He doesn't brag or sneer when he tells me that Stanley Smothers is in possession of a portfolio of half-naked girls. Many of whom are clearly underage.

"I don't find him credible," he says, "at all. He's a pedophile."

"What's that?"

"Never mind," he says.

It seems that nothing's going to happen until Mr. Wallace recovers.

Based on his story, I'll be charged with:

  a. *attempted murder*
  b. *aggravated assault causing bodily harm*
  or
  c. *accessory after the fact*

Mr. Galloway says he wants me downgraded to an accessory.

"What does accessory mean?" I say, trying not to sound sarcastic.

He looks at me over his half-glasses. I feel like he can look right through me. I can't play any games and say I'm not a handbag.

"It's one who, knowing that a party has been a party to the offense, receives, comforts, or assists that person for the purpose of enabling that person to escape."

"So comforting someone is a crime?"

"Sara, I'm just wondering what you think Mr. Wallace will say," he says absentmindedly, as if he's trying to remember a mutual friend's last name.

How the fuck should I know? I might say to anyone else. But I can't talk that way to him.

Maybe it's a mistake, but I tell him about what I did in the alley.

"Hmmm," he says, "and where was your friend when you did that to Mr. Wallace?"

He always calls Justine my friend. That's why I like him.

"She went to call an ambulance."

That's not true though. She ran off, and I waited too long and she never returned and when I went to look for her I saw only headlights and heard only a car honking back at me. She was gone.

"Did you think she was going to return?"

"I don't know," I say, because I don't know. He writes notes in his file, as I stay quiet and think about the redness that I've tried to kick out of my memory.

Redness flowed from his heart; flush after flush, red as the poppies you pin to your chest on Remembrance Day. He convulsed, once, before he moaned.

Asshole, Justine said, and I knelt down.

It was me he wanted, it was me he hated, so blame it on me.

Sara, she said, what are you doing? He's fine. Let's go.

My knife was on the pavement, lying there like a severed silver limb.

Sara, I can't stay here. He's gonna wake up soon and go home to his wife. He's fine.

She said her father was a famous poet and she wanted to find him before the police found her first. So go, I told her, just go.

I can't go to jail, she said. I'll kill myself before I go there. He'll wake up. He's alive!

I don't blame her for running. I told her to leave. The last time I saw Justine was just like the first time I saw her run in the alley. I saw her wishbone legs lift, her heels kick off the ground.

I breathed my breath into Mr. Wallace's mouth. I revived him with a drunken girl's CPR. I tore my white dress with the knife, dressed his wound, blood from his heart all over my hands, and still I pressed the white cloth tightly into his gash, a makeshift tourniquet.

I breathed my breath into Mr. Wallace though I should have run away with her and it was funny how I did that because he was after all my enemy.

*　　*　　*

My dad smuggles me white willow bark in the sleeves of his flannel shirt. He says it's a cure for fever.

He says he's planted white trilliums and they'll be in bloom for me when I go back home. He brings me all these books he said he loved when he was my age, anthropology and philosophy.

"Did they catch Justine?" I ask him, even though I know she's in Greece.

"No," he says. "That girl's like air."

I take the bark, hold it under my tongue. I don't tell Seamus that since I've been here, I haven't felt the fever. I don't want him to think I'm no longer feeling too much or fighting too hard. Maybe the cure will work in reverse and bring the hellion heat back into my civilized body.

*   *   *

I don't have time for philosophy. 'Cause Mr. Galloway brings me these black binders. He says I should read them and be prepared for what awaits me, if we go to trial, which we probably will, even though Dirk Wallace is improving, even if I'm only charged as an accessory.

Inside, there's my notebook pages photocopied. There's my mug shot on the lineup page. Me in black and white, my head cocked to the left, loose strands of hacked hair falling down. I'm in a row with tougher girls, who all look at the camera with better glares. Then there's pages and pages of cop interviews.

This stuff is called the "discovery."

I have one binder. Justine has two, and they might as well label her binders "garbage" because they're full of so many lies. I used to think slut was the worst word, but now I've found a whole new vocabulary. Antisocial, narcissistic, delusional, pathological, ADD, PCP, BYOB, who cares.

You've got to give these guys credit: they're doing their best to tell the story of my life and prove that they've got the right girl, a true-blue psychopath.

Undercovers have been working double time. What's it called? Oh yeah, overtime. I'm under arrest so they're overtime. They've even gone to Mount Doug. Got the names of my fellow students and then called them down to the station. I can see it now, the station bathroom full of girls with feathered hair and blue eye shadow, an army of Farrah Fawcett Juniors posing before the video camera as they solemnly swear to take the Bible because yeah, man, I believe in God. *Totally.*

Tiffany Chamberlain narced. I told you about her, right? My former friend turned torturess when Dean Black chose me. Well, now she's number one with a bullet on the pages of police interviews.

Sara used to be really nice. We were pretty good friends. But she was kind of a tomboy, and I guess when I became a cheerleader, we kind of had nothing in common anymore. But she was still nice. Then she started hanging out with the burnout boys. They all just hang out in the bushes and do, I don't know, drugs, I guess. A few weeks ago, she completely changed so much more. How? I don't know. She started looking really angry all the time. It was like she hated everybody. She'd just walk down the halls, giving everybody dirty looks. Now, when I look back I can see that she was plotting a murder. Do I think she's capable of hurting a total stranger? Oh my God, definitely.

The next one makes me laugh. Dave Parsons, I remember that guy. Some acned itching guy who drove a beater and got suspended once because they found him in the bathroom funneling Wildcat beer on the night of the Sadie Hawkins dance. He tried talking to me once when I was watching Ivy climb into her green Volvo. I blocked that loser out of my mind but, unluckily for me, he remembers everything.

I don't know if you guys know this but Sara grew up in some sex family. Like they were always having sex. Everywhere. Like they did it with dogs even. My pops told me all about them. They were like the Manson Family, but instead of killing sprees, they went on fuck— sorry— sex sprees. Gross hippie shit, you know. One time, oh yeah, I just remembered this the other day. One time, me and my buddies were in my car in the parking lot, and she was just hanging around. I thought maybe she wanted to talk to us 'cause she was usually back out in the bushes with Dean Black and his whole stoner crew. So, me and my friends, we weren't teasing her or nothing. We just go, "Hey, Sara, hey, is it true you were raised by the Sex Family?" And she goes, well, she didn't say anything actually. And then my friend Tommy, he was just joking, you know, he asks her if she can give his girlfriend some sex tips 'cause his girlfriend's frigid. And Sara, she just gives us this look. Cold. Like we were all laughing, but it freaked me out. You heard about her nickname right? She's psycho. We all called her the Ice Queen.

"Is Dave Parsons going to testify to that? Is he going to get up and tell everyone that I was raised in some sex family, 'cause that's not relevant. I don't want—"

"No, it's not relevant. You're right. There's only one witness I'm worried about, and I want you to read his statement and tell me if it's accurate."

Here's the one my lawyer's worried about. He says when we go to trial, this one will be quite damaging:

Mackie Hollander: I'm glad this happened. All my friends thought I was a fag because this girl attacked me and I didn't slap her. Now everyone knows she's sick in the brain. What? No, I wasn't scared. She just nicked me. Just a nick. I don't know what her problem was. I was just sitting on the bleachers with my friends and we were a little pumped up, just getting psyched, like all right, you know, we were just excited about taking on Oak Bay. Hey, is it true that she stabbed that man in the neck? Twenty-five times, that's what I heard. No, I don't know the other girl. I saw her picture though. She looks pretty weird. I don't associate with people who hang around downtown. Yeah, I'm sure it's the same knife. I have described it twenty-five times to the sketch artist, but if you really need— OK. Thanks. What was her demeanor? What does that mean? Oh, the look on her face was, I don't know, not really happy, but not scared, just like a normal girl's face. Another thing, I forgot to tell before, is that she always used to wear tomboy clothes. And that day, she dressed kind of sleazy. Like the singer in Heart or something, like she was trying to be a rock star. I don't know what color. I didn't pay her much attention.

Now, when I look back, I can see she was actually pretty crazed. She's a sicko. What kind of girl just stabs people for the hell of it? Her looks are pretty deceiving, huh? You guys must have been shocked. You should have seen her last year. She looked even more normal. I heard she was a virgin. Her girlfriends? She didn't have any. Sometimes I saw her with Heather Hale. You heard about her, right? She's messed up. I don't think Sara had a lot of good influences in her life, but that's no excuse.

Hey, I'm really sorry I didn't report this earlier, but how was I supposed to know? Locke kicked her out of school, and I thought that was good enough. But now, I'm really sorry and I feel like it's my fault, like if I'd told you guys, maybe Mr. Wallace wouldn't have gotten hurt. My mom knows some of his wife's friends, and supposedly, she's really upset and we sent her a tea basket from Murchie's.

Your partner told me I might be the star witness. Sure, yeah, wicked, I'm ready to go. I'm pretty good at public speaking. Do I have a suit? Yeah, I got one from Sears for the grad dance, but it was a rental. Oh, not a tux? Um, I'll see what I can do. Anything, you know, whatever it takes. I really want to help out you guys.

After I read that, I just keep flipping the pages. I don't want to tell my lawyer it's not accurate. Because what does it matter? You know everyone's going to believe Mackie. He's a clean-cut guy. He got his degree. Besides, I'm reading the next one.

I cry when I read it, turning my head so my lawyer won't see. This one isn't typed officially.

Handwritten, it still smells like dirt and rain.

Dear Cops,
You guys called my house fifteen times and obviously I'm not home. Get off my back. I'm treeplanting. I'm

mailing this to you cuz my foreman won't let me come down their. I know what you want to talk to me about.

Sara Shaw was my girlfriend for 7 months and 13 days. I've known her almost my entire life, since I was twelve. I'm not saying anything bad about her and my mom says I shouldn't get involved.

But I know her really well, better than anyone else. A lot of people thought she was shy but she wasn't shy, she just doesn't waste her breath on idiots. Me and her always had a lot of fun. I never even saw her hurt a fly. It pisses me off that a certain friend of mine narced to you guys about the knife. On Wednesday, she wasn't at school. Then Thursday afternoon, she showed up and that friend of mine, who you should know is a complete and total burnout, said she was swearing a lot and looking dirty and that's not like her so I don't know. I heard she's really changed so something must have happened to her. Something. She was supposed to come up here with me. I got her a job as a cook. She didn't even call. Me and Bryce waited at her house for two hours. That's why I think that something happened to her. I think that guy raped her cuz that might really screw a girl up right?

I basically ran the show in high school. I was a really popular guy and I would not go out with a PSYCHO. I liked her cuz she didn't care what anyone thought about her and I always thought she was sexy in a tough way, not like those sluts at our school who constantly giggle and are annoying little airheads. I was the only guy she'd talk to. I was the only one who could make her laugh. She just always had her own way and I thought she was really mystical, or mysterious or what the fuck. I can't believe she's stuck in a jail with a bunch of criminals. Bad shit could happen to her in there. Guys can do sick stuff. I'm worried about her.

By the way, you guys arrested my brother once for selling weed in the bushes behind Kmart. Ronnie Black. Yeah, check your files dudes. Turned out he was just possessing oregano. So you "stayed" the charges. That's cop talk for Oh, I'm sorry we made a mistake. Well, you've fucked up again with a girl and this is way different. Ronnie was 19, Sara's just 16 and you've destroyed her life. Everyone knows you guys just hassle kids when you're bored. It must be boring being a cop in a town full of fucking old people and Swedish tourists. But, you should just stop hassling kids and move to New York if you really want to fight crime. My brother can't even get a job. He's got a record since you guys haven't gotten around to saying that "stay" means oops, that weed was really oregano. My brother's on welfare. Check your files dude. Ronnie Black.

I also think you should let me talk to her cuz I hear she's not saying anything and maybe I could get her to tell the truth. I'd wear a wire and cooperate with you narcs if I could help her out. I saw it on Starsky and Hutch once. I'd be good at it. Man, I'd be AWESOME!!

I've been up here with all these lumberjacks and all I do is think about her and I've got a lot of good memories. Not that I'd ever tell you. But I could tell you that everyone else who is talking to you, like that Tiffany bitch, they're full of shit. All the girls who are saying she's crazy are just jealous cuz as soon as I started going out with Sara, all the twinkie girls stopped talking to her. Take a guess why. Now, everyone's saying Sara was always crazy. It's just bullshit. She was even a virgin and she didn't even smoke weed. I bet Mackie Hollander and his coach and ~~Shaved Cock~~ Mr. Locke are both kissing your ass because those two are major ~~assholes~~. Mackie has his whole nice guy act but he's shoved so many kids' heads in toilets his nickname is the Plunger. Ask him about that, and while you're at it, check his blood for steroids. Anyway, I don't want to narc on anyone. My mom doesn't want me to testify because she thinks you'll twist my words up and ask me if I got high. Well, yeah, I got high. So what? I still know my girlfriend. Her dad's a bit of a nut job. Last week of school, he kept calling my house looking for her and I should have known something was going on but I was cramming for exams and trying to pack and get my camping gear and everything and I just thought he was confused or she was out partying so I just told him she'd call him later. She really loves her dad though and that's another thing. If she was some PSYCHO, I don't think she'd be making sure to go home with her dad for dinner every night and being really patient with him even when he got on her nerves. There's this one guy up here who's really smart and he reads a lot of books about Russia and stuff and he says that you're basically under a lot of pressure and you can't find this punk rock psycho so you're pinning it on Sara because she's a dopelganger.

Can you tell her that I'm sorry especially for that guy raping her or whatever happened to upset her so much. And I'll always love her. Always. Always.

Yours sincerely,

Dean Black

P.S. Cops suck!!!

My lawyer says it's too bad about that last line. He was really counting on having my boyfriend testify.

They only have two statements for Justine.
The first one is from Ming.

Justine is very nice girl. I don't speak English. Sorry.

The second one is from some guy I've never heard of. He wasn't on the list of Red Zoned men.

Jack McGee: As I've told you numerous times, I met Justine at Ming's and she told me she had nowhere to go. So I let her sleep in my studio. Around seven days. She never slept. Sleeping seemed very hard for her to do. She'd slip out of my window and come back in the morning and tell me stories about how she'd met a bank robber named Athena, been to a Blue House, talked to a girl named Tahiti. I didn't believe her, but it was entertaining. On the seventh day, she tired me out. "Jack! Let's go out! Let's find a party!" I told her I was 40. We argued. I caught her tearing at her face, flinging herself around the bathroom. She knew the police were looking for her; she knew she wasn't allowed to go on certain streets. Warnings were of little concern to her. I believe after I asked her to leave, she went downstairs to Ming's. English? Yes, his English is fine. I never saw her again. An old man called a few times. He called her his little bird. I don't know his name. A physical description? Very small, skinny, five foot two, I don't know. Why would I testify? All I could say is I shouldn't have let her run but I couldn't have let her stay.

*   *   *

In my cell, I have a little cot with Sears sheets and a little desk of fake wood. I sit at the desk as if I'm a student doing homework.

The Lake of Forsaken Orphans
In the Bushes with the Burnout Boys

I write that in my notebook, then I look at the words I stole from the "discovery."

When my lawyer went to make a phone call, I ripped out the words I liked, the words I wanted to hold. Dean Black's letter, and that guy Jack McGee's last sentence about how he shouldn't have let her run but he couldn't have let her stay.

*   *   *

I wonder if Ivy Mercer is in New England yet.

When I saw all the statements by those idiots at Mount Doug, I got depressed and I told my lawyer he should try to find Ivy Mercer. She didn't really know me, I said, but you should try to find her. She always seemed really intelligent and maybe she could write something about me.

*   *   *

Nights, I read Leonard Cohen and try to distract myself from the fact that, sooner or later, I'm gonna have to narc on China and Justine.

A boy screams down the hall.

Night in juvie, sometimes I miss the sudden singe, the strange shiver.

Sometimes I want to complete the FTW that Cassie started on my shoulder.

I pick up the pencil. I touch the black point. I take off my sweatshirt and trace their secret, shared tattoo. But I can't stab it till I bleed.

Instead, the pencil moves like my dirty fingers in the garden. The pencil rises; it digs; I push it hard. And though I don't hear it, I feel like I'm singing the same soft sigh.

I write about the bushes and the burnout boys. I get lost in memory.

I'm no author, no poet's daughter, no Sylvia Plath. I just wanna distract myself from the fact that, sooner or later, I'm gonna have to narc.

If I don't blame it on Justine, they'll keep me here forever. Here. A boy screams down the hall. Shithands, they call him, he throws feces against the wall.

*   *   *

When I saw a girl slouching near the showers, I thought my malady must have returned, making me see a mirage.

But she was real, standing there, all sneaky and shy. She got caught for failure to comply.

I ran over to her, hugging her and spinning her around, and we were screaming so loud the guards almost pulled the alarm. No physical contact, ladies! Five points demerits. That's what they should have done, but I think they were so surprised by seeing me wake from my comatose state and hearing me laugh that they just let us hug. The guards aren't bad guys. Half of them say they'd be in here themselves if it weren't for a twist of fate.

Amber's dyed her hair gold; she's wrapped her braids into coils, Princess Leia style. But she still has the same plucked eyebrows and dark purple lips. The bland blue uniform only makes her face seem brighter. When she says she's smuggled in a gift for me, I think, Oh fuck no, please not the razor blades. But it's not. She's got a tiny tube of cherry lip gloss and two cigarettes. Don't ask me to tell you how she got those here. Figure it out.

As soon as I see her, I have this sudden urge to talk. Because I haven't talked to anyone here. You can't trust *anyone*, my lawyer said, don't even talk about the weather. So I've been keeping to myself, and faking sleep as much as I can. When the TV news comes on, the other kids say is it true they don't know what happened they've got no case what really happened with that dude bet he tried to rape you Justine's supposed to be crazy she's cool I met her once they call her the tiny terror what happened man and I just shrug my shoulders and say I don't remember. When that doesn't work, I say I was drunk. The only answer that shuts them up though is just saying in a low, dead voice: I don't give a fuck.

Amber! I almost started dancing a jig. I'd been so lonely. I pretty much had forgotten how to speak.

We hang out in the laundry room, blowing our smoke into the dryer.

The rinse cycle sounds like a tornado. Still, we whisper. We keep it low.

I earn cash for folding uniforms and I like the clean laundry smell. I feel a bit bad about blowing smoke onto the navy blue sweatshirts, but I don't want Amber to think I'm ungrateful for the Player's Light.

Amber says she came in here on purpose. She has something very important to tell me. . . .

But for now, we're in the laundry room, our voices hidden by the sound of washing machines.

She's still proud of her skill at entering wherever she wants to go.

"Sara, it was so easy to get into juvie. I just crossed the street in front of a cop car. Boom. 'Amber, you know you're not supposed to be in the Red Zone.' Oh really? I acted all surprised. White Oaks is full, guys. Too bad, guess you'll have to take me to juvie 'cause I'm not gonna apologize. And so I got an escort here to see you! I didn't even have to pay bus fare!"

"I really fucked up this time," I say, surprised by how nervous I sound.

I'm so confused. They keep telling me not to say anything and they say tell everything and they say the less you say the better and they say the more you say the more you dig your own grave. Shut up. Confess.

"You didn't fuck up, Sara. *They* fucked up. Besides, you don't need to worry anymore. I got something really important to give you, Sara."

"What?"

But the guard knocks on the door. "Hey, Carrie," he says. He's a big-necked buffalo who used to be a bouncer at Charmers, but he says he quit 'cause he couldn't stand the clientele.

He calls me Carrie because he saw my yearbook photo in the newspaper and he says I remind him of the red-haired girl in the movie of the book by Stephen King. I wish I was Carrie; I wish I had telekinesis because then I could cause objects to move with the mere power of my mind.

"Hey, Amber," he says. "I've got to start working harder now. I've heard about you."

*   *   *

My trial date's been set for September. I think they want to wait for the end of the tourist season 'cause a story of a psycho girl in Canada's supposedly calmest city would be bad publicity. Mr. Galloway says he's still wrangling to get my charges formally downgraded.

It's funny; it's like a play. There's a whole list of all the performers who will appear.

Her Majesty the Queen vs. Sara Shaw.

First Act.

The Crown presents their case. Starring: Mackie Hollander, Stanley Smothers, the theater students, Dave Locke, Haywood and Vowell, the Polaroid, photos of Justine's books and dresses in my bedroom, and my notebook, which they call a Diary. Dirk Wallace's doctor, his wife, his boss, his mother-in-law, and his mother.

Act Two, my lawyer doesn't want me to talk and he has no witnesses.

"Nobody?" I ask him. "Doesn't that look bad?"

"Who else should I add?" he says, chewing on his fancy fountain pen. "Help me."

"Ivy?"

He sighs. "Her mother doesn't want her involved."

Her mother just wants her to write poetry.

"Anyone else?"

Cassie and Amber, China and Heather, Dean Black and Nicholas the Skateboard Star. A sick girl with scabs on her face, a counselor nicknamed Gloria.

But I would never want those people to have to stand up before a crowd. They'd get ripped apart, embarrassed, they'd shred them all, public nuisances, cophaters, a beggar, and a dyke feminist.

Heather alone would be asked about the garden hose episode.

'Cause lawyers find out your reputation. It's fair game. Nicholas would be asked why I left his apartment and why he never took my virginity. They'll get China and ask her what she is. Solicitation for what? Speak up louder please. How many times did you OD? Please tell the court clearly as we need to understand you might be a person of bad character. Louder, louder, louder, speak up louder. Tell us how you got on your knees. You did what to Mr. Wallace? Louder, Alice, speak louder please. Tell the court and the whole world that you're a drug addict and a whore.

Just thinking about it fills me with dread. I'd die before I'd let anyone I loved go before the likes of the lady with the Picasso umbrella.

Loved, I can't believe I just said that word. Don't start thinking I'm some corny nature girl hippie.

It's funny all these people flitted in and out of my life so suddenly.

Absent on the list, they might as well not exist.

But I keep thinking about them, really, more and more and all the time.

* * *

Amber strolls around the jail waving at old acquaintances.

"Hey, Budgie, Frankie says hello."

We're in the TV room, sitting side by side. It's Movie Night. We're not allowed to watch *The Outsiders* but they'll show us *Cinderella*.

"Fuck this shit," Amber says, "meet me in your room."

We can't exactly hang out in other girls' cells. But Amber opens her hand, a finger over her lips to say ssssh, and she shows me the key pressed against the lines of her palms. You know those lines, the ones fortune-tellers read to tell you if you will marry and how old you will be when you die.

Amber knows. I don't know how. She just knows.

Maybe she remembers how I flinched when I saw her and Cassie cutting with the razor blade.

I tell her they have no idea. The cops, the lawyers, the newspaper, the people blabbing away on TV. I've tried to tell them but I wouldn't know where to start. They'd need songs for their report; they'd need to see The World by Alice, a finger tasting father's gin. And even then, would they ever understand?

And while I sleep, I let her read my new notebook. All I've got so far is Chapters One and Two. She reads what no one else ever will. In the Bushes with the Burnout Boys. It's not relevant. In the rainsoaked bushes where I lay back and wished for a crown of twigs and moss.

"Hey," she says, waking me from dream like she used to do when we were roommates at the home for disturbed girls.

I'm dreaming nightmares of Queen Elizabeth letting loose a white tiger to tear open my striped face.

But Amber's real. She takes the key from her underwear, smiles triumphantly. "Hey," she says, "when you write about White Oaks, you better not forget that I told you I've got the gift. Remember me. I'm a motherfucking Houdini!"

When it's that time, I'm ready.

I've been brought a blue dress with a lace collar. Wardrobe for my preliminary hearing.

That's where we have a rehearsal for the trial. All witnesses please arise and proceed to describe Miss Shaw as a violent liar who, even before the incident, carried a knife around. In her bra!

I pull the dress on and look at myself for the first time in days or weeks. Days or weeks I've been in here, and in that time my breasts and hips have returned, fuller than they were before, as if I've gone through some postfever puberty. My face is framed by red bangs; the rest of my hair reaches below my ears, fading white at the tips. Freckles cover my cheeks as if I'd been sun-kissed. Will they recognize me from the photo in the newspapers? I look nothing like the fake, smiling girl in the Mount Doug yearbook. Do I look like the girl people envision when they read the newspaper articles and hear me described as troubled and naive?

I'm not worried. 'Cause I look like I'm falling in love for the first time. I'm pretty positive no one will recognize me.

I hope you don't hate me for what I'm about to do. That's your problem, I guess.

I trick myself: I'm going somewhere I belong, like Chinatown in New York, a place where there's veering streets and crowds of people rushing around their exciting, thrilling lives.

Pull the sweatpants over my dress, stick the new notebook in my waistband. Too bad about the flip-flops, but Amber says shoes aren't necessary.

In my cell, I draw a heart in pencil. It's corny, but who cares? It's the best I can do.

The guy in the kitchen has a crush on Houdini. Plus, she's non-chalant. "Hey, buddy, your hot dogs are awesome. Got any cucumbers? I wanna do this mask thing 'cause I read that it gets rid of the bags under your eyes. Yeah, yeah, I got permission. Just one cucumber, please pretty please."

Last night, she unlocked the door.

I slip toward the door, pretending I'm thin as Justine.

Sometimes it comes in handy to be ignored. And today is one of those days.

As the doors open, Amber and the kitchen guy have their backs to me. She's got him searching through the freezer.

Then, I'm jumping off a ledge—pretending I'm Nicholas, knees to my chest as I perfectly execute my little three-quarter revolution.

Oh God, thank you; thank you, Everly.

Garbage bags of teenage criminals' waste, that's what cushions my fall.

She gave me a map, but I don't need to check it 'cause I've memorized the lines.

There's no guard dogs or search tower outside of the hick town juvie in this pretty town.

There's just a parking lot shared by employees of the Capital Health Region District.

Through the Toyota Corollas and Subarus, over the yellow lines, and by the Reserved for the Handicapped signs.

Onto a street, past a corner grocery store with a handmade sign saying: LOTTO JACKPOT TICKETS ARE NOW HERE!!!! GET READY TO WIN!

When I'm in the forest, I strip off my sweat suit and lie back for a while, just looking up at the evergreens. Sooke is so far from the small city. I'm surrounded by the familiar smell of Christmas and rot and rain.

*   *   *

I'd love to say there's a happy ending like in some dumbass movie. Dean Black comes driving down in his Trans Am, head out the window, bellowing, *We are the Champions*. Justine sends down a helicopter, and I'm whisked away to meet her famous father on the island of Crete. Everly is waiting in a chauffeured limousine.

But it's just me leaving the forest and walking down dark gravel roads until I reach a construction site. There's the skeleton frames of new houses and the smell of concrete. The sign's already up. COMING SOON: THE CHANTICLER MANOR. Chanticler Manor! Fuck off, this is the wilderness.

Down by the soon to be cul-de-sac, there's a dirt road full of roaches and Bacardi bottles. From the dirt road, I can see a paved road stretching along, bordered by evergreens, it leads down to the gray valley of the highway. The dress is too tight along my thighs; I rip it with my hands so I can run faster if I need to 'cause I might. I don't even know where I'm going. I'm just heading along the road, hitchhiking. Cars pass; it starts to rain. A beat-up car passes me and I hear stoned laughter, the screams of AC/DC. *Back in black. Yes, I'm back in black. Number one with a bullet; I'm a power pack.* If Ivy Mercer was here she'd write a poem about the mist rising over the mountains, the hopeful road that opens up before me, but I don't notice the beautiful things. I stare at the beater and see a faint face looking back at me. I can barely see her face. She's hidden by steam on the glass. Maybe steam from her boyfriend's breath, maybe from pot smoke, maybe the constant fog. That girl in the backseat of the beater, I wonder if she's bored and restless, stuck in this small town, hating the slow, stoned laughter and the same rock song on the radio. I hope she caught a glimpse of me through the steam. Even if she only saw my tear widen and my legs kick off the ground, she might think I know where I'm going. She might think I've found a way.

ACKNOWLEDGMENTS

Thanks to my family, Karen Hanson, Iris Tupholme, Felicia Quon, Nikola Scott, Dan Conaway, Emma Parry, Byrd Leavell, Janet Johnson, Heather McGowan, Juliette Consigny, Fi Campbell, Michael Turner, Patrick Li, Eli Langer, Jeff Rogers, Louise Dennys, Alex M., Dean M., Julian M., Jesse Jr., and ever for J. C.